"You might as well come in."

Jen stabbed her key toward the lock.

"Stop!"

Tyler's sudden bellow froze Jen to the spot. The man stepped up behind her and pulled her to himself with one iron arm.

"What?" She started to resist.

"Stop." The softer hiss was more urgent than his shout.

He pointed toward her doorknob. Her eyes widened. A wire as thin as gossamer and nearly invisible wrapped the knob. Then he traced the line with his pointer finger up to the overhang of the walkway above. Her gaze followed his finger and came to rest on a claylike square object stuck to a wooden beam. A metal prong poked out of the clay with a small light blinking like an evil red eye at its tip.

A bomb. And opening her door would have set it off.

Jen had heard the expression about the blood freezing in a person's veins and had considered the phrase a bit of hyperbole. She stood corrected now that the phenomenon had turned her to icy stone.

Jill Elizabeth Nelson writes what she likes to read—faith-based tales of adventure seasoned with romance. Parts of the year find her and her husband on the international mission field. Other parts find them at home in rural Minnesota, surrounded by the woods and prairie and their four grown children and young grandchildren. More about Jill and her books can be found at jillelizabethnelson.com or Facebook.com/jillelizabethnelson.author.

Books by Jill Elizabeth Nelson

Love Inspired Suspense

Evidence of Murder
Witness to Murder
Calculated Revenge
Legacy of Lies
Betrayal on the Border
Frame-Up
Shake Down
Rocky Mountain Sabotage
Duty to Defend
Lone Survivor
The Baby's Defender
Hunted for Christmas
In Need of Protection
Unsolved Abduction
Hunted in Alaska
Safeguarding the Baby
Targeted for Elimination

Visit the Author Profile page at LoveInspired.com.

TARGETED FOR ELIMINATION

JILL ELIZABETH NELSON

LOVE INSPIRED SUSPENSE

INSPIRATIONAL ROMANCE

LOVE INSPIRED® SUSPENSE
INSPIRATIONAL ROMANCE

ISBN-13: 978-1-335-59933-9

Targeted for Elimination

Recycling programs
for this product may
not exist in your area.

For questions and comments about the quality of this book, please contact us at CustomerService@Harlequin.com.

Love Inspired
22 Adelaide St. West, 41st Floor
Toronto, Ontario M5H 4E3, Canada
www.LoveInspired.com

Printed in U.S.A.

Our soul is escaped as a bird out of the snare
of the fowlers: the snare is broken, and we are escaped.
Our help is in the name of the Lord,
who made heaven and earth.
—*Psalm* 124:7-8

To the family members who deal with addiction
and its consequences. May your courage and strength
be continually renewed.

ONE

The soles of Jen Blackwell's running shoes slapped rhythmically against the dirt path as she tackled an incline along a wilderness trail through the Great Smoky Mountains National Park of Tennessee. Pine-scented morning air filled her lungs, and a pleasantly cool mountain breeze kissed her cheeks. On either side of her, tendrils of damp fog undulated between the trunks of aspen and maple trees that were in the first full leaf of spring. Birdsong and the rustles of small creatures in the undergrowth accompanied the puff of her breath. This early in the morning, with the sun barely peeking over the horizon, Jen had the path to herself—precisely the way she liked to experience the peaceful wild before starting her busy day as a newly minted detective with the Gatlinburg Police Department.

A shriek tore the serenity, followed by a gurgling rasp. Jen skidded to a stop, her skin prickling. No forest animal made a cry like that. Only one creature could produce such a sound. She strained her ears to make out any further indication of human presence. Nothing. Even nature had gone eerily silent, as if holding its collective breath.

Jen's heart thudded against her rib cage. Where had the scream come from? Not from within the trees on either side of her or the path behind her. Someone not far up the trail but out of sight had let out a hideous cry and then gone stone-quiet.

Drawing a deep breath, Jen took a tentative step forward and then halted. She was alone and miles away from civilization, with no means of knowing who or what lay ahead. Had a mountain lion or a bear attacked another runner? If so, surely there would have been animal snarls and growls to go with the human shriek. Possibly someone had cried out while taking a fall. She should see what she could do to help.

Jen moved forward, not running but striding cautiously now. The skin of her arms tingled beneath the lightweight, long-sleeved hoodie she wore. Normal forest sounds resumed, ratcheting down her alarm. She rounded a bend in the path and spotted a bulky form crumpled on the ground in the middle of the pathway.

Jen hurried forward. The person lay perfectly still, not twitching a muscle at her approach.

On a catch of breath, Jen stopped mere feet from the still body of a paunchy man lying on his side and dressed in a suit and shiny shoes—the opposite of wilderness attire. The incongruence barely registered with Jen as her gaze fixed on the arrow sticking out from the man's chest. A chest that had ceased rising and falling.

Someone had shot the guy with a bow and arrow. An accident, possibly? Some bow hunter mistaking this person for a deer? Jen shook her head. This balding man in thick glasses and neatly knotted tie bore no resemblance to a four-legged creature of the wild.

Jen dropped to her knees and pressed two fingers to the man's neck and then to his wrist. Not a whisper of a pulse from either location. She hadn't expected one. The marksman had sent his arrow cleanly through the victim's heart.

Every hair on Jen's head prickled. Was the killer gone or even now nocking an arrow with her in his sights? Jen sprang to her feet and lunged toward the trees.

Z-z-zip! Something streaked past her shoulder and *thwapped* into the trunk of a nearby spruce.

Heart in her throat, Jen stumbled, lost footing on a loose rock and then toppled full length onto the loamy earth. The impact drove the breath from her lungs. Pain encompassed her suddenly vacant chest cavity, but Jen ignored the discomfort and forced her body to roll off the path and down the slope into the cover of the trees. The sudden fright had lent extra impetus to her movement, and the incline exceeded her expectations, sending her into an uncontrolled tumble, bouncing like a pinball off tree trunks and large rocks until abruptly she flopped to a halt, splayed like a rag doll in a bed of ferns at the bottom of the hollow.

At last, blessed oxygen filled her lungs, but she released the inhalation with a long groan. The arrow may have missed her, but the immovable objects in her uncoordinated escape path had left aching bruises on her arms, torso and legs. Gingerly, Jen attempted to move her limbs. Everything responded with only minor protests. No broken bones.

Thank You, Lord!

Harsh reality crashed into her brain—a murderer lurked in the forest above. One that had already taken a life and intended to make her his second victim.

Move, Detective Blackwell.

Jen rolled onto all fours, then rose into a crouch, even as her hand sought the pancake holster at her side. Her fingers closed around the butt of her Glock 22 service weapon. She never left home without it, a habit she'd learned the hard way. The familiar ache of loss gripped her throat, but she swallowed it. No time for old nightmares. She had a killer to catch.

Drawing the Glock from its holster, she began to creep uphill, moving from cover to cover behind trees. Her gaze swept the area as her ears strained for any sound foreign to the woods. If the deadly archer lurked above, she meant to ambush him. Or her. A savage growl simmered in her belly, but she refused its release from her throat. Her daddy had taught her well from childhood how to move soundlessly in the woods. If—no, *when* she took him to the church service on Sunday in the care facility's lovely chapel, she would thank him.

At last, she drew nearly level with the pathway, yet she remained under cover and out of sight from anyone observing it. Slowly, pistol held in a two-handed grip, Jen swiveled her body in increments from left to right, a move called slicing the pie. No sight, no sound of human intrusion in the wilderness save for herself and the still body on the ground obliquely to the right of her position. Tension eased from Jen's muscles.

There!

A flash of blue between the trees on the far

side of the path. Her finger tightened around the Glock's trigger, even as her mouth opened to deliver the cop's warning to surrender.

"Hold it right there," ordered a stern voice to her rear. "I've got you covered cold. Put the weapon down."

Every muscle in Jen's body froze. How had the killer gotten behind her? And what was that glimpse of something blue she'd seen on the opposite side of the path? Some kind of decoy? The flesh between her shoulder blades tingled. Would an arrow soon bury itself there?

"You don't want to do this." She swallowed her amazement that her voice emerged firm and strong when her insides were quivering. "I'm a detective with the Gatlinburg Police Department."

"Jennifer?" The baritone voice had gone tentative. "Jen Blackwell?"

Jen's jaw sagged open as her arms weakened and her weapon slowly lowered. Could her ears be deceiving her? It couldn't be! She eased herself around to face the man who held a hunting rifle that was now pointed toward the ground. No bow and arrow in sight, so he wasn't the killer. But in her earlier life, he'd been something almost as devastating.

He stood taller than she remembered and with broad shoulders filling out the park ranger uniform he wore. Not the endearingly gangly teenager she'd known. And he sported a thick but neatly trimmed dark beard and mustache beneath the vivid blue eyes that had once captured her heart—before he ripped it clean out of her chest.

"Tyler Cade," she pronounced in a tone that hammered each syllable.

For her, the choice of response to this man she hadn't seen for fourteen years—since the day they'd graduated high school together—was either going to be anger or tears. At least the former preserved her dignity.

Tyler's head swirled, and his heart bounced around in his chest. What was Jen Blackwell doing here in his forest, waving a handgun around like she meant to use it on someone? Handguns were not wildlife hunting weapons. But then, she'd said she was a cop with the Gatlinburg PD.

"Is there some fugitive in the park that the rangers haven't been notified about?" He finally regained control of his tongue, if not his scattered thoughts. He stepped up closer to the path, his gaze scanning the area. "And what would a city cop be doing out here going after one?"

"Get down!" she snapped, frowning at him as

she ducked into a deep crouch. "There's a murderer around here shooting arrows at people."

Tyler gaped at her. Not only because of the outrageous nonsense she had spouted but because this woman was the last person he'd expected to see today—or any day—and she'd morphed from unformed adolescent cutie to sculpted stunner in the decade-plus since he'd last seen her. Those green eyes sliced into him like lasers. Then she lunged at him and tackled his legs like an award-winning linebacker.

Flailing in the air, Tyler toppled to the ground. A sharp projectile whizzed past his wide-eyed gaze even as he hit the ground. She hadn't been kidding about the archer.

"Let's go get this guy," Jen snarled as she scrambled off him, taking a businesslike grip on her pistol.

Tyler rolled to his side, spotted the rifle he'd dropped during his trip to the ground and snatched it up.

"I'll take north," he said between gritted teeth. "You take south. We'll flank him."

She jerked a nod and melted out of sight into the trees.

Tyler squelched a grin. Jen hadn't lost any of the woodcraft she'd learned growing up deep in the Appalachians. Neither had he.

Throwing off the remnants of his astonishment at meeting his childhood friend and once-upon-a-time sweetheart out here under these extraordinary circumstances, he threaded his way forward in a soundless crouch. It was possible their quarry had already fled. If only Tyler had Dixie with him on his rounds this morning, but she was at home nursing her six-week-old pups. The bluetick coonhound would have ensured the guy couldn't slink away undetected. Then again, Tyler wouldn't have been eager to risk his dog's life going up against an armed criminal.

He reached the path but remained under the cover of a thick tree trunk. Tyler's skin prickled at the sight of a crumpled body on the path visible in his peripheral vision. And the guy was dressed in a business suit, no less—an unexpected twist for sure.

Tyler frowned. Getting across the open path without taking an arrow from the assailant could be a challenge. Slowly, he picked up a fist-sized rock from the ground. He hurled it away from himself as a noise distraction, then darted across the dirt track into the cover of the trees on the other side. No arrow greeted his movement.

Tyler went still and sucked in a deep breath laden with the odors of loamy earth and blooming wildflowers. His sudden activity had suspended normal forest noises, but as he stood frozen in place, birdsong and the chitter of a nearby squirrel resumed. Tyler crept onward, moving smoothly as glass between the trees, the soles of his hiking boots soundless against the soft mulch beneath his feet.

At last, he spotted Jen squatting near the base of a yellow buckeye tree in full flower. She seemed to be studying something on the ground. Her hair, caught back in a ponytail that flowed down past her shoulder blades, was nearly the same shade as the tree's lush golden panicles. Though Tyler had made no sound, Jen's head lifted, and she met his gaze with a grim expression.

"I believe our bowhunter is gone. But he took his shots from this spot."

He drew closer, and she pointed at the impressions in the earth that betrayed something heavy lurking there over a long period of time. He read the marks not as a pair of footprints but as a single footprint of a man-sized hiking boot on one side and a knee and tip-of-the-toe combination on the other. Someone had knelt here in a stable pose of one knee down and the other leg bent with its foot flat against the ground to maintain balance—an excellent position for any marksman.

Tyler squatted beside Jen but instantly regretted the proximity. Clearly, she still liked that spicy floral-scented shampoo that was quintessentially *her*, which used to make his pulse beat faster. He swallowed. Used to? Not hardly. She still had the same effect on him.

He wrenched his thoughts away from swarming memories, most of them good and wholesome and wonderful. But then there were other memories, especially those at the end—

Squashing the despair that attempted to rise in his heart, he trained his gaze in the direction that would have been the archer's view from this vantage point. The location provided a generous space between the trees toward the path and beyond, affording an excellent line of sight and lack of obstruction. The body of the suited man lay within that area.

"Who has law enforcement jurisdiction inside a national park?" Jen's eyebrows lifted.

"I do…well, the United States Park Service Rangers do. And I'm a ranger." He swiped the radio from his utility belt. "I'll have to call for additional help to investigate a murder and attempted murder."

"Not too common out here, I would guess."

Tyler shook his head. "Hunting accidents? Unhappily, yes. But outright murder, not so much."

He pressed the communications button on

his radio, and Lynsey, the dispatcher, soon answered. "This is Tyler Cade," he told her and then gave her his location coordinates. "We need a team of crime scene investigators out here and assistance from as many rangers in the area that can be spared. We have a murder scene to contain and investigate."

Pregnant silence fell at the announcement of a murder.

Then the dispatcher cleared her throat. "I'll have ranger assistance coming your way shortly." Lynsey's tone remained professional despite what must have been a shock. "As soon as I've called in for the CSIs, I'll let you know their ETA."

"Thanks, Lyns. We'll need transport for a dead body, too." He ended the radio communication and gazed into his companion's intense eyes. "Let's back away from this location as delicately as possible so as not to disturb the scene any further."

Jen nodded, rose and faded with seamless efficiency into the forest, heading toward the path. Tyler followed her like a noiseless wake. They stopped together on the track a dozen feet or so from the body.

"Have you touched him?" Tyler motioned at the still figure.

"I approached to see if he needed medical

assistance. There was no pulse at his neck or wrist, and he wasn't breathing, so I didn't try CPR. When I stood to move away, the archer shot at me. Then I stumbled and fell into the ravine."

"You're not hurt in any way?"

Tyler scanned her clothing for blood and spotted a few raised scratches on her hands and one on her cheek, but her long-sleeved hoodie and leggings prevented him from observing any other potential damage. He hadn't noticed a hitch in her stride or any favoring of her arms, so no bone breaks or sprains, evidently.

"I'm fine, Tyler." Her tone conveyed dry exasperation. "And, no, I don't recognize the guy who got shot."

One side of Tyler's mouth flickered upward. With her characteristic quickness, she'd preempted his next question. A pang shot through his gut. How he'd missed this person's presence in his life, but he hadn't acknowledged the extent of the Jen-sized emptiness inside him until now, when she'd suddenly reappeared. Too bad there was no fixing what had happened. What he'd had to do. Even if there were the slightest chance she'd understand, he had pledged to himself never to tell her why he left town without a word all those years ago. The knowledge would shatter her world.

Tyler swallowed against a dry throat. "What time do you need to report in for work?"

Jen consulted a small gold watch on her wrist. "Eight a.m., and I need to shower and change. I'd barely make it even if I left this second."

"Go." He jerked his head toward the path down the mountain. "I've got this."

"Don't be a knothead, Tyger." Color splashed across her high cheekbones. Probably embarrassment at her careless lapse into using his old nickname born of her inability to say his name correctly when she was the toddler who lived next door.

"I'm not moving until your backup arrives," she continued, ignoring her own faux pax. "Then I suppose you'll want a full, formal statement, though I don't know what to add to what I've already said." The color receded from her face, leaving it pale as snow around taut lips thinned to a pencil line. "Except I thought I detected a flash of blue between the trees at the moment you came up behind me. Could the attacker have been wearing blue or carrying something blue?"

"Good question. Are you sure you weren't looking at a clump of wildflowers?"

"Definitely not. I know the difference between organic and synthetic. This was not a natural phenomenon."

Tyler frowned. "Blue would not be a logical choice for hunting apparel."

"True. Orange would be typical if the hunter wanted to be seen and differentiated from wildlife. Olive drab, brown or a mix of the two would be the choice if the hunter wanted to blend into the landscape."

"And what about this guy?" Tyler motioned toward the body. "There are no offices out here requiring a suit."

Jenny shrugged. "As is true with a lot of investigations, we start with more questions than answers. Though I have to say this scenario is weirder than any I've come across."

"How long have you been a detective?"

"I was a beat cop for most of a decade in Nashville." Her gaze scanned the landscape in any direction but his. "Then I took the classes and passed the exams to become a detective. There were no openings for the position in Nashville, so I interviewed and got the job in Gatlinburg. This is supposed to be my first day." She glanced toward him, wearing a rueful smile.

"Yikes! Welcome to the neighborhood."

Her musical chuckle burst forth and played havoc with Tyler's pulse rate. That sound had taunted him in his dreams for years. He never thought he'd hear it again in real life.

"I'd better call and let them know I'll be late and why." Jen pulled a cell phone from a fastener on the band around her slender waist that also supported her pancake holster and pistol.

He frowned. "I'm sorry you got caught up in something like this on your first day on the job."

Her gaze met and held his for long seconds. "Me, too." She stepped away to make her call.

Tyler's heart went hollow. Was she sorry only about the murder, or did she wish she hadn't bumped into him? If only he could convince himself her regret applied strictly to the former. Whatever scenarios he'd ever considered that might bring him into contact with Jen again, finding a dead body and investigating a murder had never been a remote possibility.

A frown formed on his face. After eliminating the victim in the suit, it was odd that the killer had not made his escape but lurked in the forest to shoot at them. To shoot at *her* first. What did that mean? Tyler's arrival at the scene could not have been anticipated, but if Jen regularly ran this route, the archer might have been lying in wait specifically for her.

Tyler's chest tightened in realization. Jen might still be a target.

TWO

Standing in the shadow of a maple tree and keeping her head on a swivel, senses alert for any nearby intruder, Jen placed a call to her shift supervisor at the Gatlinburg PD, Captain Stuart Mackey. He didn't pick up, so she left a message outlining her situation in broad strokes. Then she called the dispatcher on duty to inform the PD of her status and that she'd be in as soon as she was able to leave the scene. The duty officer sounded suitably concerned and promised to pass her message along.

With a deep sigh, Jen tucked her phone into the holder at her waist and turned her gaze on Tyler, who had squatted on the trail and was scanning the ground for clues. The corners of her mouth drooped. *Why, God?* Why had she abruptly encountered this man again just when her career was taking off amid a looming family crisis? She didn't need this complication in the mix.

The buzz of an engine from up the trail drew her attention. Moments later, a four-wheeled ATV hove into sight, with a husky, gray-haired male in ranger uniform driving. A second engine sounded behind her, and she turned to find another ATV rolling toward her from the path below. The second ATV stopped near her position, and a tall, svelte, dark-haired thirtysomething woman in a ranger's uniform stepped off the vehicle.

"You must be the witness." The dark-haired woman met Jen's gaze with skeptical brown eyes. "Some guy in a suit got shot with an arrow out here for real?"

Jen motioned up the track to where the body lay. Beyond the deceased, Tyler and the male driver of the other ATV had come together at the side of the trail. Tyler was talking and gesturing toward the body, and then he turned and pointed into the woods. He must be telling the other ranger about the site where the archer had lain in wait. The CSIs would no doubt want to make a cast of the boot print.

The female ranger's gaze was fixed on the suited victim. She let out a whistle under her breath. "Ty is DI law enforcement trained and authorized, so I imagine he'll be leading this investigation. I don't envy him the task."

"DI law enforcement?"

"Department of the Interior. Not all rangers have the additional designation, but Ty's background in the military police made him an ideal fit for the position here. Didn't require much extra training."

The military. Jen narrowed her gaze on Tyler's tall, sturdy figure. Was that where he went after he disappeared from her life, their hometown and everything they'd ever known?

Jen returned her attention to the woman standing beside her. "I'm Jen Blackwell, a detective with the Gatlinburg PD. I was out here for a morning jog before starting work when I came across this."

"Rachel Tarrant." The woman hardly glanced Jen's way. Rachel's entire focus had settled on Tyler, and a soft smile played on the woman's full lips.

Jen's gut clenched. Either there was a romance going on between Tyler and Rachel, or Rachel aspired for them to be a couple. Whichever was the truth, it was none of Jen's business, and best she remember that fact. Jen could no longer trust Tyler—at least, not with her heart. Good thing her feelings for her teenage sweetheart were long dead. And she'd keep telling herself that for as long as it took to believe it.

"Tyler," she called to him, and he turned

around to meet her gaze. "Your backup is here, so I'm going to head to my car and get on in to work."

"Where is your car?" Brow knitted, he walked toward her, skirting the death site.

"In the parking lot at the base of the trail a couple of miles back."

She frowned toward the suited man lying motionless on the trail. If the guy's point of origin was the same as hers, he'd trekked a long way in attire that would be uncomfortable for the environment. What if his vehicle was in the same parking lot as hers?

"I'll drive you down on one of the ATVs." Tyler stopped a few feet from her and offered Rachel a nod of acknowledgment. But his gaze quickly returned to Jen. "For one thing, turnabout is fair play. You didn't want to leave me alone until backup arrived. Now I don't want to let you go back to your car alone. The archer could still be lurking somewhere in the trees. Also—"

"You want to check the lot for the victim's car." She finished the sentence for him.

"Great minds." He grinned at her.

Involuntarily, Jen grinned back, her heart doing a backflip. *No, no, no!* Charming her could not be that easy. She stifled the smile and blanked her face.

She shrugged. "Have it your way."

A shadow of something—regret?—passed over Tyler's expression, and he sobered. "The archer may also have parked in the same lot. Do you remember seeing vehicles other than yours when you pulled in?"

Searching her memory, Jen lifted her gaze to study the steadily brightening blue sky above the hiking path. Too bad the sun was shining down on such a sinister scene on this fresh new morning.

"I remember only one vehicle in the lot other than mine."

"Let's go check it out." Tyler headed for the ATV Rachel had driven up in.

Jen followed him, choosing to ignore the dark glare she glimpsed on the female ranger's face. Hopefully the woman would soon figure out she had no cause for jealousy. Not that it helped achieve the goal when Jen would have to climb onto the ATV behind Tyler and wrap her arms around his waist while they drove.

Apparently oblivious to the byplay, Tyler handed Jen a helmet and then fitted his own on his head. Or maybe not so oblivious, because he waved toward Rachel as he climbed onto the ATV.

"The scene is in your capable hands. You

and Greg make sure no one gets close unless it's the CSIs."

Rachel beamed like he'd told her she was the most beautiful woman on the planet. Which she nearly was. Scowling, Jen turned away as she strapped on her helmet. If Tyler weren't already enthralled by his coworker, he surely would be soon. And that was all for the best, right?

Jen's head proclaimed a hearty amen, but her heart whispered something quite different. Good thing she'd trained herself to listen to her head. The other way around was a recipe for hurt, as she'd learned all over again recently. A pang of loss smote her for the second time this morning. Taking the job in Gatlinburg to ascend to detective status more quickly than in the larger city was only one of the three big reasons she'd been eager to relocate. But no one here needed to know any details of her life in Memphis.

Firming her jaw, Jen climbed onto the ATV behind Tyler and woodenly gripped his belt on either side.

He looked over his shoulder at her. "Better take a firmer hold than that. The trail can be bumpy."

Suppressing a sigh, Jen surrendered to the expedient and wrapped her arms around his waist. The position, with her nose so close to Tyler's neck, would be more bearable if he'd had the courtesy to change his soap since they'd last been this close. But no, he still smelled of suede leather with a buttery sandalwood undertone. The special soap was Tyler's one slightly costly indulgence from his meager paycheck as a teenager helping out part-time at the feedstore. He'd claimed he bought it for her, and she had appreciated it. Reminiscent images of happy times swarmed through Jen's head as if she was viewing them through a glass marred by the anger, hurt and bewilderment of his sudden departure from the small Appalachian town they'd grown up in together.

The ATV's engine revved, and they were underway. At least the engine noise would forestall any necessity for conversation. And once Jen was on her way back to Gatlinburg, there would be little reason for Tyler and her to continue encountering one another. She'd simply have to find another place to take her morning runs and put his presence in the area out of her mind. Easy to decide, no doubt more difficult to achieve, but she meant to succeed.

Although they traveled at a sedate pace, the tree trunks seemed to fly past on either side of the track. Tyler was correct about the bumpiness under the tires. She winced as they went over a stray tree root. Within a quarter of an hour, they emerged from the tree line into a grassy verge bordering a parking lot. Tyler slowed the vehicle and Jen sat back, her gaze sweeping the paved area. Her little red Mazda remained where she'd parked it, with the black Buick sedan she'd noticed when she arrived at the park still occupying a slot nearby.

Tyler stopped next to the Buick. "Is this the vehicle you saw this morning?"

"It is." Jen climbed off the ATV. "My car is over there." She motioned toward it, then furrowed her brow. "Do rangers give out parking tickets?"

"Sometimes."

"Was I parked illegally or something? I made sure my slot was not marked reserved in any way." She moved toward her vehicle where a piece of paper flapped in the breeze under the windshield wiper.

"There would be no reason to issue a citation on your car where you're parked." Tyler's voice came from close on her heels. "Besides, the paper is too big for one of our tickets."

Jen reached the Mazda and snatched the sheet from under the wiper. On a plain white piece of copy paper, someone had drawn a crude archery target with an arrow sticking out of the bull's-eye. Scrawled underneath were the words *Next time I won't miss.*

Next time? The breath stalled in Jen's chest, and her blood ran cold.

Evidently the deadly archer still had a target painted on her. But why? If they knew the answer to that question, the murder might already be solved. Worse, now the killer had rendered it impossible for Jen to simply go and do her job in Gatlinburg and let the rangers do theirs at the park. A death threat ensnared her in this investigation with Tyler whether she liked it or not.

"Hang on to that sheet of paper right where you have hold of it. Don't touch it further. Here comes our crime scene techs." He nodded toward the bulky, white van with lettering on the side that was turning into the parking lot.

"Techs from Gatlinburg?" Jen's gaze shot question marks at him.

He shrugged. "The park service doesn't have CSIs on staff. We pull them from surrounding communities when we need them."

"I suppose that makes sense."

Tyler waved toward the van, which then headed in their direction. As soon as the vehicle stopped, a middle-aged woman riding on the passenger side climbed out and approached them. Tyler asked if she would bag the note from the killer and get it logged into evidence. The threatening page was soon secured. Jen flapped her hands as if the note had burned her fingers. Mentally, that was probably what such a message felt like.

"I need to get going."

"Wait, Jen." Tyler lifted a forestalling hand. "We'll first need to let the investigators dust for prints on the windshield wiper, the glass of the windshield and the car chassis."

Jen's shoulders slumped. "I'd better let the department know I'm further delayed."

"Tell them about the threatening note, too."

She shot him a sour look but jerked a nod as she pulled out her phone and took a few steps away from him. Tyler understood. A cop never liked being cast as a potential victim even though the dangers of their daily job perpetually put them in that position.

Tyler got on the radio and asked Lynsey to run the plates of the Buick sitting in the parking lot and find out who owned it. As he ended the communication, a trio of vehicles entered the parking lot. One was a park service pickup. Another was a state highway patrol vehicle, light bubbles whirling but no siren. The third was an ambulance with its lights off. A thin older man hopped spryly from the ambulance, professional bag in hand. The medical examiner. Two other uniformed individuals exited the same vehicle—the emergency services personnel who would have to trundle the body manually down the trail on a stretcher and whisk it away to the morgue once the remains were released by the ME.

Tyler grabbed one of the evidence techs, the man who'd driven the van, and they converged with the medical examiner as he headed for the trail. Tyler assigned the tech to take his evidence collection kit and transport the medical examiner up the trail on the ATV. Then they were to send one of the rangers back with the ATV to transport the other evidence tech to the scene. By then, the latter tech should be done processing Jen's car.

Next, Tyler moved on to the pair of highway patrol personnel and asked them to cordon off the entrance to the parking lot and prevent any civilians from entering the area. Lastly, he approached the stocky man in a park service uniform who had climbed out of the ranger service truck.

Jen fell into stride beside him. "Busy around here for this early in the morning."

"Not the kind of busy we like."

"Agreed."

Tyler shook hands with the man who'd exited the pickup, then turned his gaze on Jen. "This is Lamont Jacobs, the park manager and also my boss."

"*Usually* the boss." A deep chuckle left Lamont's barrel chest. "In criminal matters, I defer to Tyler. And you are…" He let the question trail away as he offered his dinner-plate-sized hand to Jen.

Her dainty fingers were engulfed by his. "Jen Blackwell. I was jogging this morning, came upon the scene and called it in."

"What she hasn't mentioned," Tyler put in, "is that she's a detective with the Gatlinburg PD, and the killer took a shot with an arrow at both of us. Jen basically saved my life by knocking me out of the way of a crossbow bolt that had my name on it."

"Crossbow bolt?" Jen blinked up at him. "I had been picturing a longbow like we used to use."

Tyler shook his head. "There's a significant contrast in weight and size between a crossbow bolt and a longbow arrow. The former is shorter and heavier. I recognized the difference."

"Ah." Her expression went flat. "You never said."

Tyler bit back a spurt of exasperation. There hadn't been time for a technical discussion. But

Jen never did like to feel uninformed about anything. Probably a great characteristic in a detective, but the trait must have made his sudden disappearance extra galling to her on top of her personal hurt those many years ago. Tyler gritted his teeth. If he'd been able to do things any other way back then, he would have.

"Thank you for looking out for my ranger, Detective Blackwell." Lamont tilted his head toward her.

"Don't mention it. Call me Jen, please, sir."

"And I am Lamont."

The pair smiled at each other pleasantly, even though the stiff shoulder Jen turned toward Tyler radiated chill.

The park manager switched his focus to Tyler and frowned. "If some creep is slinking through the forest shooting bolts at people, how concerned should I be about the visitors to our park? We're entering the busy season."

"It's too soon to say there is widespread danger. Certain bizarre characteristics of the crime suggest this was a targeted killing…and I mean no pun by that statement."

"I agree with Tyler," Jen spoke up. "There is nothing random about this situation. I'd be shocked if this were the start of an indiscriminate killing spree."

Lamont's posture relaxed even as Tyler's

went rigid. Nothing random about this situation? Jen's words—probably unintentionally on her part—magnified the horrifying possibility he'd already been considering. What if the murder of the man in the suit was staged for Jen's benefit with her as a target all along? The note on her windshield underscored the validity of the speculation.

The radio on Tyler's belt crackled and he jerked. His boss eyed him with a raised brow. Tyler lifted a placating hand and swiped the radio from his belt.

"Cade here."

"You wanted to know the owner of the Buick," Lynsey answered. "It's a guy by the name of Arthur Gillespie. Lives in Gatlinburg. He's—"

"My father's financial advisor!" Jen's exclamation drowned out Lynsey's voice.

Tyler stared down at the woman beside him. "His financial adviser? Since when did Jarod Blackwell, general handyman and bluegrass banjo picker extraordinaire of Mount Airy, North Carolina, come to need a financial advisor?"

Jen smirked at him. "Since a mother lode of emeralds was discovered practically in our backyard seven years ago. Remember that acreage we own a few miles from our place?

The one with the interesting rock formations? The formations were hiding a major secret until a rockfall caused by erosion brought a few sparkly green gems to the surface."

Speechless, Tyler gaped. She reached up a finger and closed his jaw for him.

He shook himself. "I thought you said you didn't recognize the victim?"

"I didn't. I'd never met him, but I know the name and have spoken to him on the phone."

Lamont let out a loud hum. "The connection between your family and the victim certainly supports the theory that the killer targeted Mr. Gillespie and, by extension, you."

Tyler's heart sank. His boss had come to the same dismaying conclusion that he had. Jen was in danger.

His radio crackled again. He'd forgotten he'd left Lynsey hanging in their conversation.

"I'm here," he told her. "Sorry for cutting you off. Thanks for the information, but I've got to go." He put the radio back on his belt. "Could this case be about your family's emerald mine, Jen? Greed is a common motive for murder. Since you're an only child and your mother passed away years ago, I assume you would be first in line to inherit."

"Yes, I would."

"Who would be next?"

Jen's face washed white. "My father!"

"No, not your father." Tyler suppressed an eye roll Jen must be more rattled than she let on. "He's the principal."

"He could be in danger." She whirled and hurried toward her car.

Tyler's gut twisted as he caught on. If obtaining the inheritance was the motive, the perpetrator would also need to eliminate the senior Blackwell.

He loped to catch up to Jen. "You can't mean to drive to North Carolina. Wouldn't it be quicker to phone the Mount Airy Police Department to go check on him?"

She pulled her key fob from the pouch on her belt. "Dad moved to Gatlinburg right after the emerald discovery made it financially possible. He grew up in this area. Mount Airy was my mom's home turf." She skidded to a halt by her driver's door. "I've got to go now."

"Not alone." Tyler placed his hand against the door latch.

"Don't worry. I can call the Gatlinburg PD for backup. You're needed here." She brushed his hand aside.

He backed away, grinding his teeth. She was right, but everything in him champed to stay by her side. Helplessly, he watched her pull out and race from the parking lot, barely allowing the state troopers to open the barricade they'd placed across the entrance to the parking lot.

Tyler's hands balled into fists as her vehicle disappeared from view. He'd never forgive himself if something happened to her or her father now. Preserving their family intact was the whole reason he'd left their hometown so abruptly fourteen years ago.

He'd vowed to take the secret to his grave. But now? No. He shook his head. There was no way those old events could tie into the current tragedy. He'd snipped those threads. Hadn't he? Yet if he was wrong, the motive of simple greed connected to the emerald mine paled compared to the twisted darkness of bitterness and revenge that may have erupted from the past.

THREE

Jen mentally kicked herself as she raced down the highway. She should have let Tyler come with her. Being late for work with a solid cause was one thing, happening upon a murder being as solid as reasons came. But calling her new place of work with what might sound like a hysterical request for protection for her only remaining close family member could quickly make her a joke in the department, especially if her father turned out to be perfectly fine.

Please, God, let him be fine.

Her phone rang, and her onboard screen showed her a number she didn't recognize. Should she answer? Probably. With her change in job and locality, there were many people with numbers yet unknown to her who could legitimately call her. Over time, she'd connect numbers with names.

Then a thought froze the oxygen in her lungs. What if it was the killer?

She slowly released the pent-up breath. If the archer were reaching out to her, having obtained her cell number by some nefarious means, she *really* needed to answer. Steeling herself, Jen pushed the button to open the connection.

"Hello." At least her voice didn't shake like her hand was doing.

"Jen."

A buoyant sensation flowed through her. Not the killer.

"Tyler, how can I help you?"

"Things are going smoothly here in capable hands. My personal presence isn't necessary on-site. It's more a matter of waiting until test results start coming in. Give me the address where you're going, and I'll meet you there. I need to talk to you *and* your father."

Jen gulped down a lump that was trying to form in her throat. "I don't know. It will be a shock for him to see you. He's not well."

A soft gasp came through the connection. "What's the illness? Not cancer like your mother, I hope."

"No, not cancer. For the past two years, he's been battling ALS, also known as Lou Gehrig's disease. Lately, the debilitating process has accelerated. His failing health is one of the reasons I wanted—no, *needed*—to work in Gatlinburg. He's in an assisted living home, and we don't know how long he's got."

"All the more reason for me to talk with you both as soon as possible."

How could a human voice convey certainty and insecurity at the same time? Tyler's tone managed the feat. Jen's insides clenched. What did he need so badly to say? One way to find out. She gave him the address of the assisted living home.

"I'll see you there. Use caution and be vigilant."

"Of course." She ended the connection.

Her lips thinned, and her jaw firmed. That man had lost all right long ago to give her any advice. Even if it was good advice. She pushed the irritation to the back of her mind. Ensuring her father's safety was all that mattered. She had another fifteen minutes on the road ahead of her. Any backup she could have called in from the local PD wouldn't arrive much more quickly than that. Still, every moment counted. She pressed down on the accelerator.

Why had she thought it was a good idea to drive the twenty miles to the Great Smoky Mountains National Park to jog every day for the past week since she'd moved to Gatlinburg in preparation for starting her job? There were parks in the city where she could have gotten her exercise. But those parks weren't secluded and close to nature, elements she'd sorely missed during her years in Memphis.

Somehow the killer archer had known where she'd be this morning and had set up his scenario accordingly. That meant she'd been under surveillance for some time and hadn't even felt the hostile eyes. Disappointing and dismaying. Her situational awareness was usually very high. Then again, maybe she *had* sensed the observation but hadn't differentiated the feeling of being watched from the strangeness of everything in a new environment. Either that or the watcher was very good. Or perhaps a combination of both factors.

The point was moot now, though. A man had been killed, she was threatened and her father might also be in danger. If it took collaborating with Tyler Cade to stop the criminal from wreaking more havoc, she'd have to suck it up and soldier on.

At last, the outskirts of Gatlinburg drew her in, and she navigated to the Silver Meadows Assisted Living Home on a quiet street in a good neighborhood. The single-story, stone-fronted building appeared as peaceful as it always did.

What were you expecting, girl? A sign out front announcing Crime in Progress?

The usual number of cars sat parked in the employee lot, though the visitor area was nearly bare this early in the morning. The only visitors likely to be present would be family members sitting overnight with a dying relative. Jen parked her vehicle in a slot as close as possible to the canopy shading the front entrance. She hopped out onto the pavement, then stood still for several moments observing and breathing the spring air. A faint honey-like scent from the white blooms of a nearby forsythia bush touched her nostrils, but no sense of being watched twanged her nerves.

Jen stepped through the entrance and helped herself to one of the complimentary nose-and-mouth masks presented for visitors in an attractive wicker basket on a table inside the front door. Ahead of her, a pleasant-faced, gray-haired woman she recognized sat behind the reception desk.

The woman looked up from her paperwork, and the deepening wrinkles at the corners of her eyes indicated a smile behind her mask. "Hi, Jen. You're here bright and early to see your father. I'm not sure he's even up yet, much less has eaten breakfast."

"Hey, Olivia." Jen struggled to keep her tone relaxed. "Has anyone else been in to see my father?"

Olivia's brow furrowed at the odd question. "Not yet this morning." She tapped the keys on her computer and eyed the screen. "No one since you visited last night."

"Good." Tension leeched from her shoulders. "I'll go peek in on him."

Should she alert the staff to her concerns about her father? Jen mentally shook her head. There was no evidence beyond speculation that any danger existed.

"Sure thing." Olivia's breezy wave toward the hallway gave no evidence that the nurse picked up on Jen's tension.

On her way toward her father's room, Jen passed busy staff members with carts visiting the cozy, private suites that housed the residents. The aides would be getting their charges up, dressed, fed, and supervising their medication intake. Jen's dad had been requiring more and more assistance with activities of daily living, as well as needing oxygen through a nasal tube 24/7, especially at night when lying prone. Not much more time would pass before hospice qualification would be in order.

Jen's stomach roiled. She was far from ready to say goodbye to her only remaining parent. *Not fair, God. Not fair.* Then again, life was not fair—she knew that well. As her mom had taught her, at times like these the best a person could do was lean deeper into the Everlasting Arms for comfort and assurance, though Jen wasn't feeling much of either at this moment.

Her jogging shoes made almost no sound against the commercial-grade carpet beneath her feet until she came to her father's door to find it fully closed. The aides had not yet reached his room this morning. Jen turned the knob and let herself into silent darkness. The level of illness in this ward rendered it inadvisable to allow the occupant to lock any doors when quick access could be necessary at any given moment. The encroaching state of dependence on such an independent man as Jen's father had become increasingly chafing for him.

Jen stopped and listened. The soft hiss of the breathing machine wafting from his bedroom was a good sign. She flipped on an overhead light and crept softly through the tiny living room to the bedroom door, which hung slightly ajar. No cause for alarm. All signs normal. She could turn around and leave right now, but she wanted to look into the room, hopefully without waking him. Her skin prickled, not with alarm but because she hated feeling like a sneak where her own father was concerned, but his health and well-being had to take precedence over privacy.

Silently, she pressed the door a few inches farther open and slid her body into the room. Standing stationary, she let her eyes adjust to the dimness. The figure in the bed lay stone-still. Jen's gaze traced the translucent oxygen tubes from the breathing machine toward her father's head on the pillow and came up short. The cannula was not in his nose. Her dad might have pulled the tubes out overnight, but then an alert should have sounded at the nurses' station. Someone had removed the tubes and shut off the machine's alert function. And now her father didn't seem to be breathing by himself.

With a cry, Jen flipped on the overhead light and then darted for the bed. She pressed the general alarm button to summon help. With shaking hands, she snatched up the cannula and fitted it where it belonged in her father's nostrils. He did not begin to breathe. She felt his neck. The flesh was warm, and a pulse throbbed faintly beneath her fingertips. At least his heart was still beating. He couldn't have been without oxygen long.

"C'mon, Dad, breathe!" She positioned his head and opened his mouth so he could receive timed puffs of air from her own lungs.

She'd been at it seemingly forever but probably only for a minute or so when staff arrived to take over. An aide gently pulled Jen's quaking body away from the bed as the professionals went to work.

"Jen, what's going on?"

She whirled toward the familiar voice from the living room. Tyler stood there, tall and sturdy as an oak. With a sob, Jen ran to him and flung herself into strong arms that wrapped her and held her close.

"Someone got to him. I know it. Someone—"

"Shh-shh-shh." The arms rocked her. "It'll be all right. I promise."

I promise? The words washed over Jen like a dash of cold water. This man's promises had lost all credibility years ago. What was she doing in his arms while her father's life hung in the balance?

Jen stiffened in Tyler's grasp, and he knew the reason. Why had he impulsively blurted a promise concerning circumstances he had no control over and had no way of delivering? She already viewed him as untrustworthy. Jen pulled away from him, and he let her go.

Stone-faced, she brushed at the moisture on her cheeks. "Thanks for coming, Tyler, but I'm all right, and the medical staff is looking after my father. You can—"

"Ms. Blackwell." The soft address spoken

by an aide cut off what Tyler assumed would be a dismissal.

Jen whirled toward the young woman, scarcely more than a teenager, who was wringing her hands and shifting her weight from foot to foot.

"My father. Is he—" Jen's question stopped on a gulp as she visibly paled.

"No, not that." The young aide touched Jen on the arm. "They've got him breathing again, but he's unresponsive. We're going to transfer him to the hospital for tests. We don't know how long he was without oxygen."

"I'm going to ride with him in the ambulance."

"Of course."

Tyler stepped closer. "I'll follow. Then when you're ready to leave, I can bring you back to get your car."

Jen frowned up at him. "Don't worry about transportation for me. I can always call for a rideshare. However long it takes, I'll be by my dad's bedside until he's evaluated and stabilized. Hopefully, when he wakes up, he can tell us who sabotaged his equipment."

"That answer is bound to be pertinent to the murder investigation and the threat against you. Too much of a coincidence if it wasn't."

"I agree. I should get someone from the

Gatlinburg PD to start interviewing staff to see if anyone saw who accessed my father's room."

"I can get started with that."

Jen shook her head. "This crime occurred in the city, not in the park."

Tyler offered her a half grin. "My jurisdiction is federal, but I'd like to work with the PD. Cooperation will get us farther faster."

"Right." She let out a huff. "Let me put you in touch with my captain. I need to call him anyway and update him on the situation."

"Why don't you let me do that, too? I think the ambulance is here." He nodded his head toward a pair of uniformed EMTs wheeling a gurney into the room.

"Thank you." Her gaze toward him softened, then she abruptly turned away and moved closer to the action around Jarod Blackwell.

Tyler retreated to a corner where he initiated a call to the Gatlinburg PD headquarters. While the connection went through, his gaze followed the loaded gurney out of the room. In the doorway, Jen turned and afforded him a nod. Then she followed her father into the hall.

Tyler's gut churned. As reluctant as he was to speak with the man again or even be in his presence, he desperately needed Jarod's input in finding out whether ancient history was revisiting them with deadly vengeance. Hopefully without Jen in the room. How he was going to pull that off, he had no idea.

Please, God, let Jarod wake up and be lucid.

On the other hand, this whole thing could be about inheriting the emerald mine. In that case, digging up ancient history wouldn't be necessary. The secret could stay buried. But at what cost? Now that Jennifer Blackwell had reentered his life, could he stand to lose her again? Yet, exposing the truth about his abrupt departure from their hometown would hardly endear him to her. It might even put the nail in the coffin of any hope of rekindling a relationship.

A soft growl left his lips even as his call was picked up. Tyler was soon put through to Captain Stuart Mackey. The guy spoke with a gravelly voice that suggested a long-term smoker. Tyler updated him on the twist the murder case had taken, the threat toward his detective, which he already knew about, and the attack on her father. When he finished, silence fell for several heartbeats. Tyler let the man mull the situation over.

"I suppose you think you're the lead investigator on this case," the man finally said.

"I *am* lead, but I'd rather have the PD with me on this than bring in additional federal agents and go around you. This is your town, and, if I'm not mistaken, the deceased victim is a citizen of Gatlinburg."

"I like your attitude." The tone carried cautious approval. "You've already involved my CSIs, so we're covered there."

"Much appreciated. Would you send them here when they're done at the park? A small army of medical staff have already traipsed through Jarod Blackwell's room, but we might as well be thorough."

"Will do. I can also send a pair of officers to help interview personnel and, if necessary, residents at the care center. I'll have one of my detectives link up with you."

"If I may make a suggestion, you already have a detective involved."

"Well, now, it would be irregular to assign a detective who's a witness and has a family member as a victim."

"I can do irregular. She has a high stake in catching this creep and making no mistakes about it."

The captain harrumphed. "Have it your way, then. But I expect to be kept in the loop at all times."

"My exact intentions."

They concluded the call, and Tyler tucked his phone away in his shirt pocket. Jen wouldn't be thrilled to have to work closely with him on this case, but she'd be devastated if she was excluded from the investigation.

Tyler left the room, located one of the aides and had her block the door with a spare cart until the uniforms arrived to help sequester the scene for the CSIs and to conduct interviews. Then he sought out the charge nurse for the day. The round-faced, middle-aged man was in his office behind his desk.

The nurse frowned as he stood and offered his hand to Tyler. "I'm Decker Browne."

Tyler introduced himself and took the seat offered to him by the charge nurse. Decker then resumed his seat behind the desk and steepled his fingers.

"An unhappy event this morning. I imagine you'll want to interview staff, so I'll make them available."

"That would be appreciated. What time is the shift change in the morning?"

"Shift change starts at seven a.m. and is complete by seven thirty. There's a half-hour overlap of personnel so updates on our residents can be exchanged."

The timing rang alarm bells in Tyler's head. The archer would have had to be in the forest already at that hour. Did the killer have a helper who did the dirty work here at the care home? Nasty prospect. Tyler tucked the thought away for later examination.

"During shift change," he said to the charge nurse, "would a stranger be able to slip through the kerfuffle and access one of the suites?"

Decker's frown deepened. "Highly doubtful." He looked away and made a show of straightening a few papers on his desk, probably musing on the possibility of a lawsuit.

"But not impossible. Wouldn't staff notice an unfamiliar employee or visitor?"

The man sighed and met Tyler's steady gaze. "We're not open for visitors until eight a.m., so a random person in street clothes before that would be noticed immediately. But as to personnel, you have to understand that staff turnover among aides in care facilities can be quite high."

"So a new employee in the mix wouldn't be thought odd."

"Not right away."

"Do you have surveillance cameras on the premises?"

"At the entrances and in the hallways. Our residents wouldn't like surveillance in their apartments."

"Understandable. Please send copies of the footage from the entrances and the hallway leading to Mr. Blackwell's unit to this email address." Tyler handed Decker one of his business cards.

"What time frame would you like the footage to cover?"

"An hour or so before the morning shift change until now. Mr. Blackwell's equipment hadn't been sabotaged long before Jen arrived here."

"Okay. Let me see."

The charge nurse turned toward his computer and began tapping keys. Suddenly, his expression went sour.

Tyler stiffened. "What is it?"

"It appears our cameras went offline at six thirty a.m. and came back on again at seven a.m."

"Right when shift change started, but not during."

Wide-eyed, the nurse shook his head. "No, not during."

Tyler rubbed his bearded chin. The earlier time frame made it barely possible that whoever had sabotaged Jarod Blackwell's oxygen was also the archer from the woods. But it raised another question.

"If Mr. Blackwell's oxygen had been removed that early in the morning, wouldn't he have been long dead before his daughter arrived?"

Decker shook his head. "Not necessarily. Mr. Blackwell *is* still able to breathe on his own. It's simply becoming more difficult for him, especially when lying down. It might have taken some time for his respirations to cease."

"Wouldn't struggling to breathe have roused him to call for help?"

"I would think so, but—" The nurse spread his hands.

Dread pooled in Tyler's gut. What if removing the oxygen cannula was a decoy—something that would account for Jarod Blackwell's death but wasn't the real threat? What if he'd been injected with something or given something slow-acting that was spreading throughout his system, and getting him breathing again was only temporary? No one at the hospital, including Jen, would know to look for a life-threatening substance in his bloodstream.

Tyler leaped up and strode out of the charge nurse's office. Grabbing his phone, he put through a call to Jen's phone. She didn't answer.

Gritting his teeth, he headed for the front door and nearly bumped into a pair of uniformed officers coming in. In terse sentences, he explained that he needed them to secure Mr. Blackwell's suite for the CSIs and start conducting interviews with staff on-site to find out if anyone had noticed any strangers in the facility—including new staff members—and if they'd seen anybody entering the victim's unit. The officers said they understood, and Tyler charged for the park service pickup he'd driven into town.

As soon as he got on the road toward the hospital, he tried calling Jen again but received only voice mail. He left a plea for her to call him as soon as she got the message. He considered ringing the hospital's general line, but the rigmarole of getting through to someone who could act on what was little better than a hunch on his part would take him longer than arriving on their doorstep in person, where he could be much more persuasive.

Minutes later, outside the hospital's front door, Tyler screeched to a halt, the pickup chassis rocking on its springs. He leaped from the cab and was about to charge into the building when strange, violent movement nearby in the parking lot caught his attention. A hulking male swung his fist toward a familiar female head sporting a long, blond ponytail.

Tyler's breath caught. Jen was under attack.

FOUR

As the hamlike fist rammed toward her face, Jen twisted to the side, and the human bludgeon swooshed harmlessly past her head. The displaced air blew like wind in her ear. Unbalanced by his own fruitless momentum, the ruffian staggered. Seizing the advantage, Jen's instinctive martial-arts moves sent the attacker to the pavement, where he lay curled up and groaning, attempting to cover his gut with one arm and massaging his throat with the opposite hand. So much for an overgrown bully. Clearly the guy had relied purely on his size for so long that a capable response from a smaller person caught him off guard.

"Whoa!"

Jen's attention jerked toward the deep-voiced exclamation.

Tyler trotted up to the scene, sharp gaze darting from her to the man on the ground and back again. "You sure Krav Maga-ed him into submission." His tone was half-admiring and half-dismayed.

Jen planted her hands on her hips and rolled her eyes. "Leave it to you to turn the proper title of a self-defense technique into a quirky verb." She'd forgotten the offbeat sense of humor he tended to manifest during tense moments.

"I'm quirky enough to have these." He fished zip ties out of a pocket and knelt by the downed assailant "Guess what? You're under arrest for assaulting an officer of the law."

"Officer of the law!" the guy squeaked through a throat still recovering from Jen's incapacitating blow. He glared up at her. "You're just some la-di-da chick in a designer jogging outfit."

Tyler snorted as he applied the zip ties. "Goes to show the clothes do not the detective make."

Jen returned her attacker's glare. "Detective Jen Blackwell. You're under arrest for assault, and since you seem to assume I've got money, we'll throw attempted robbery into the mix."

"Robbery!" The guy scowled as Tyler hauled him to his feet. "I wasn't supposed to steal nothin'. I—" The man clamped his jaw shut as if he'd said too much.

"Someone put you up to this?" Tyler shook the man's arm.

Jen quickly interjected with the Miranda warning. "*Now* you tell us who sent you."

"Leave this guy with me, Jen." Tyler's tone was urgent. "You can trust me to ask the pertinent questions. How is your father?"

Jen blinked against hot tears suddenly welling. "Fighting for his life. He can't breathe on his own. They've got him hooked up to a ventilator. I stepped out here to use my cell phone in privacy to update my captain, and then this joker pounced." She motioned toward the subdued criminal.

"I'll take care of the update when I turn this guy in. Right now, you need to get back into the hospital and warn the medical staff that they could be dealing with an incapacitating drug in your dad's system."

"A drug!" Her heart stuttered in her chest.

"Think about it. Unless he was drugged, how did his assailant mess with his equipment without Jarod resisting or crying out? And why did he lie there seemingly unaware he was struggling to breathe?"

Jen clapped a hand over her mouth and then drew it away. "Why didn't I think of that?"

"It took me a while to think of it, and I'm not as distracted as you are. Go!"

Jen turned and raced back into the hospital as if she were being chased by a pack of wolves. Once inside, she fitted her face mask on as she moderated her pace to a power walk so as not to knock someone down. But she maintained a brisk pace, except for the brief ride in the elevator, until she reached the intensive care area where her dad was located. Immediately, she hustled to the nurses' station and asked to speak to the attending physician on an urgent matter about a patient. Thankfully, the nurse she spoke to didn't offer any obstructions or fish for more information but paged the doctor immediately.

Less than a minute later, a petite, gray-haired woman in a white medical jacket strode toward her. "I am Dr. Ashraf. What seems to be the problem?"

"I'm Jen Blackwell, a detective with the Gatlinburg police. My father Jarod Blackwell was brought in because of a sudden respiratory arrest. Though he has ALS, he's been breathing well enough with the aid of continuous oxygen. Early this morning someone removed his oxygen while he slept. It isn't like my dad not to react to an intruder in his room. We believe he may have been given a drug to sedate him and keep him from responding or realizing his oxygen had been removed. Has his blood been tested for any type of sedative?"

The doctor's dark eyebrows climbed toward

her hairline. "We hadn't thought to look for anything like that since the ALS alone could be causing his symptoms. We can run the test right away." She turned and gave the nurse the order for the blood draw, and the woman hustled away. "We still have Mr. Blackwell on a ventilator because he struggles to breathe on his own. A sedative in his system could well be hampering his lung function. Thank you for bringing this to our attention. What made you think of this possibility?"

Warmth crept through Jen's limbs. *Bless you, Tyler.* "A quick-thinking law enforcement colleague suggested the idea. If you discover a sedative in my dad's bloodstream, will you be able to give him something to counteract the effects, and will that help him through this crisis?"

The corners of the doctor's eyes crinkled, indicating a smile beneath the mask. "Yes, to the first question and quite possibly to the second."

"Thank you, Doctor." Impulsively, Jen grabbed Dr. Ashraf's hand and gave it a gentle squeeze.

The woman squeezed back, offered a kindly nod and then hustled away up the hall.

On dragging feet, Jen returned to the waiting area where she'd been skulking after they first arrived at the hospital. She wasn't allowed to sit with her father until they stabilized him. Sitting still didn't seem possible. She was too wired. So she paced, and time dragged along with no word.

"I'm surprised there isn't a groove in the carpet by now."

Jen turned toward the source of the familiar voice to find Tyler gazing at her with compassionate eyes that counterbalanced his mildly teasing tone. She had to consciously force herself not to rush to him like she'd done when he arrived at her father's assisted living suite. What was it about this guy that felt synonymous with comfort and safety? He'd abandoned her without explanation. She should loathe him, but more's the pity, she didn't. Quite the opposite, but she couldn't let him see that the old attraction still existed.

Jen drew herself up stiff. "No word, yet, about the blood test results."

"Give the medical staff time to do their job." He stepped deeper into the waiting room and lowered himself into a cloth-covered armchair.

She let out a huff and plopped into a chair opposite him. "I know it hasn't been long, but to me it seems like it's taking forever."

Tyler consulted his watch. "It's been less than a half hour since you were assaulted in the parking lot."

"Feels like a century ago. What have you done with my assailant?"

"Made a call, and your colleagues with the Gatlinburg PD came and hauled him away."

"Did the guy explain why he went after me? Or who hired him?"

He rippled his shoulders in a shrug. "Babbled something about being paid to do a simple job roughing up a woman. Only he used a rather nasty slang term instead of 'woman.' He stonewalled on the name of who hired him or why, but I figure if he sits in a sterile police interview room stewing on the consequences of his actions for a while, he might be more ready to talk in an hour or two."

Jen sat forward, elbows on knees. "I want to be in on that chat."

Tyler shook his head. "I doubt they'll let you participate. You're the victim."

She crossed her arms and sat back. "I at least want to observe the conversation."

"We should both do that because it would be a strange coincidence if this incident didn't tie into what's going on with the dead financial advisor and the attempts on our lives and your father's life."

"Agreed."

Dr. Ashraf's slight figure popped into view.

She halted at the entrance to the waiting room, a somber expression in her eyes.

Jen's heart seized in her chest. *Dear Lord, please don't take my father. Not yet! And not like this, the victim of a murderer.*

Tyler's gut clenched. All color had drained from Jen's cheeks, and the doc's face didn't broadcast encouraging news. He offered up a silent prayer for God's strength to fill Jen and carry her through whatever happened. His faith had been milk-toast sloppy before he went into the military. The things he'd seen and done on active duty had forced him to either solidify his trust in God or abandon it. He'd chosen the former and had never regretted the decision to lean into the Almighty instead of pulling away. No matter what.

"Ms. Blackwell, could we step into my office? I have an update."

"My father." Her voice came out choked. "Is he…?"

"He's alive." The doctor spoke briskly. "But we should talk details in private."

"You can speak in front of Tyler. He's investigating the attack on him. What did you find?"

"Very well." The doc shot a sidelong glance toward Tyler. "We found fentanyl in your father's system. We've administered naloxone to counteract the effects of the illicit substance, and his vital signs show that he is responding to treatment."

"Does that mean he's going to be all right?"

"It's too soon to say. He hasn't awakened yet. The strong opioid has given the ALS an advantage. We'll have to wait and hope for the best."

"Hang in there, Jen. Your father is a fighter. He'll beat this."

Tyler's jaw tensed as he clamped his mouth shut. Where had those words come from? He wasn't given to sugarcoating tough circumstances. Life had taught him better than that. But the anguish on Jen's face had wrung his heart. Now he was spouting platitudes he had no idea the future would deliver. Still, from the look of gratitude Jen sent his way, Tyler couldn't regret his words.

The stiffness in Jen's posture seemed to melt away. "May I go sit with my dad?"

The doctor nodded. "I think that would be a good thing. Talk to him a little bit, hold his hand and let him know he's got someone pulling for him to recover. At least as much as is possible given his preexisting condition."

"We can do that." Jen stood up, her gaze falling on Tyler.

His heart gave a little jump. "You want me

to come with you?" His question emerged laden with uncertainty and tainted with dread.

Did he really want to spend time in Jarod Blackwell's presence again after what had happened all those years ago? A surge of anger heated his gut, but he tamped it down, along with the heat. What was the matter with him? He'd been so sure he'd left those hard feelings behind. Then again, his dutiful determination to be forgiving had never been tested by proximity to the man until now.

Jen's sharp gaze sifted him, and her eyes narrowed. "You don't want to come along?"

How was she interpreting his obvious physiological symptoms of reluctance? Did she think he was experiencing guilt? As if the long-ago estrangement was *his* fault? If so, he could hardly correct her now. Probably not ever.

Tyler willed the tension to leave his body, and he unspooled the fists that had formed involuntarily. He dredged up a smile—well, the shadow of one anyway—that he hoped conveyed through his eyes since his lips were hidden behind the mandatory mask.

"Sure, I'll come with you and look in on him, but I can't stay. We do eventually have to interview him, but it doesn't sound like that will happen anytime soon. You should sit with him as long as you like, but I have to leave the hospital and follow up with people on the progress of the murder case. Hopefully we have some results from the evidence collection at the park. It'll probably be a while yet before we have much to go on from your father's room."

"If anything." Jen snorted. "Whoever is behind all this is devious and innovative. I can't see him leaving us a nice set of fingerprints on my father's nasal cannula or breathing machine."

"I hope you're wrong about that, but it's a faint hope. Your description of this crook seems spot-on."

Her gaze locked with his, and in her eyes, the steely determination of a seasoned investigator replaced the trepidation of a family member concerned for a loved one. "We're going to catch this guy. For now, I'll do as you say and spend some time with my father. Hopefully he'll wake up soon, and we can interview him together. But if not, I'll leave him in the capable hands of the medical professionals and get back to work. The best way I can serve my father is to expose who's out to kill him."

"And you." Tyler uttered the reminder gently but firmly.

"And me." She conceded with a nod. "We won't be safe until we have the culprit behind bars."

"I want you safe, Jen. It's what I've always wanted." The words blurted from Tyler's lips before he could stop them.

Jen winced as if he'd poked an open sore. "I won't pretend to understand what you mean by that statement."

Tyler's gaze fell to the toes of his hiking boots. The explanation for what must have sounded to her like a hypocritical pronouncement remained locked behind his lips.

She led the way out of the waiting room into the hallway. The doctor had moved on to carry out her duties elsewhere and was not in view. Tyler followed Jen into a private room in the intensive care unit. Jen moved quickly to her father's side while Tyler froze stone-stiff just over the threshold.

The ventilator machine hissed and puffed, breathing for the slack figure in the bed. What little of Jarod's head remained visible outside of the straps and the bulky plastic mask revealed pasty, gray skin stretched over bony cheeks and topped by wisps of grizzled hair. The body beneath the sheets was a shrunken shadow of the vigorous, burly man Tyler had known. He swallowed a lump in his throat. He'd occasionally daydreamed about an air-clearing confrontation between Jarod Blackwell and himself, but not under these circumstances, with the man clinging to life by a fingernail. What should he feel now instead of anger? Pity?

Jen gripped her father's limp hand and turned toward Tyler. He quickly blanked his expression, which might betray his conflicted hostility toward her father.

"I know he looks terrible. The ALS has carried him downhill in a hurry this past year, but before the onset of the disease, Dad was sturdy and strong and lucid the way he used to be before Mom died. You never got to see it, but after you left, it was like someone flipped a switch, and he quit drinking. He became his old self again, except for the sadness that never entirely went away."

Jen's gaze accused him of bailing out on her before her father's marvelous recovery, thus sacrificing what could have been the restoration of great relationships, not only between him and Jen but between him and her father. If only she knew how much he'd craved a return to the surrogate fatherhood Jarod Blackwell had given the orphaned Tyler when he was a boy growing up under the care of an aging grandmother. Grandma had passed away only a few months before he graduated high school, and he really could have used the support Jarod used to offer.

But that bond of respect and affection between Tyler and Jarod had evaporated years before—when he and Jen were in the ninth grade and Julie Blackwell, Jen's mom, died quickly of an aggressive cancer. From that point on, Jarod devolved into a bitter man who lived for his next drink and locked everyone out, including his own daughter and the teenage boy who had placed him on a pedestal reserved for good fathers. The hurt he'd received as a young man was unfathomable and, to Tyler's dismay, apparently remained unresolved to the present day.

He reined in his emotions. There was no time for if-onlys or dealing with old, ill-healed wounds. Sure, he was glad to hear Jarod had gotten himself back on track and become close with his daughter again after he left Mount Airy. That much was an answer to prayer. But it was too late for him and Jarod to do the same. Reality was what it was, and he had a murder case on his hands, plus the attempted murder of Jarod Blackwell, and the ongoing threat hanging over Jen's head. Unless the past had something to do with the present danger, secrets should stay buried.

Heart in turmoil, he turned and left the hospital.

FIVE

Jen sat holding her father's hand, mentally examining her interaction with Tyler since they'd encountered each other in the woods. What was the man hiding from her? His occasional furtive mannerisms and the fleeting expressions he failed to suppress fully indicated an inner disturbance he wasn't willing to share. Whatever it was seemed to connect with her father. Could something have happened between them before Tyler abruptly left Mount Airy? How could that be?

Dad had never indicated ill feelings toward Tyler after the young man disappeared. If anything, he'd spoken only well of Tyler, even though Dad's heart must have been hurt, too, by his sudden desertion. Dad had urged Jen to let Tyler go "find himself," as young men so often needed to do, and to cling to the good memories while her heart healed and someone new came along to fill the void. Her father had been sure that in time she'd be able to move on from Tyler and find another love. After all, Dad had assured her, high school romances rarely led to anything permanent.

Her father had been partially right. The pain had faded though it never disappeared, and she'd dated other guys in college, although nothing ever lasted. Maybe what felt like a massive rejection and betrayal from Tyler had tainted her ability to trust another romantic relationship. That is, until Grant, her partner in the Memphis PD.

With him, she'd started to feel whole again. Not that they'd even so much as gone out on a date. That sort of fraternization would have been frowned upon between partners in the department. But they'd spent all day every workday in each other's company. An easy friendship and an intuitive camaraderie had developed so that they could practically read each other's thoughts. Much like it used to be with Tyler.

Jen had begun to entertain the notion that she *might* possibly fall in love with Grant, and he with her. If that happened, they could no longer be work partners, but maybe they'd have something better than that. Maybe. The big question mark over the implications of committing her heart to Grant held her back from discussing with him her growing feelings toward him, even though she sensed his developing romantic interest in her, as well. Then the botched robbery and ensuing shootout happened, and a bullet from a desperate criminal's gun destroyed any prospect of a future with Grant.

With the loss of her partner, the old feelings of abandonment had rushed back quadrupled. Not that he'd had any control over leaving her, like Tyler surely had possessed. She shouldn't, couldn't blame Grant for getting killed. Yet, perversely, like grief sometimes worked, a part of her sometimes felt angry with him. Only by throwing herself into her quest to achieve detective status and moving away from Memphis had she avoided a total emotional shipwreck. Now, when her career goals were on track and a new start was before her, Tyler had reappeared in her life as abruptly as he'd left. Plus, he'd returned when she was emotionally vulnerable, coping with her father's terminal illness.

Not fair, God. Not fair at all.

Her father's hand twitched in hers, and Jen sat up stiffly, with a gasp. Her gaze flew to her father's face. His facial muscles were still slack, but did his skin color seem a bit healthier, and did she detect some eye movement behind his closed lids?

"Dad?" The word crept softly between her lips.

No response. The movement behind the eyelids ceased. Had he been dreaming? Did that mean he might be coming out of his coma? With his next breath, the lift of his chest seemed more robust, as if he were helping the machine draw air into his lungs.

Jen depressed the call button to summon the nurse. Then a knock at the door brought her head around. That was no nurse poking his head into the room but one of the officers she'd met at police headquarters during her orientation.

The twentysomething guy offered an uncertain smile. "The captain sent me to stand watch outside your father's room. He said there was a threat."

"Excuse me." A brisk female voice spoke from behind the officer.

The young man stood aside to admit the nurse. Jen outlined to her the slight activity she'd noticed in her father. The nurse pursed her lips and nodded her head, then said she'd have the doctor stop in soon. Jen trailed the woman's exit as far as the doorway. The young officer she remembered as Rod Jones, nicknamed Red because of his hair color, had taken up a post in the hallway next to the entrance to her father's room.

"I'm grateful to Captain Mackey for thinking about offering protection," she told him. "Someone made an attempt on my father's life."

"No problem. But it wasn't Cap who first thought of it. Some federal cop with the National Park Service urged the idea, and Cap caught right on. So here I am."

Jen gritted her teeth against a spike of irritation. Why did it bother her that she had Tyler to thank for the additional security? Maybe because she wasn't ready to forgive him for skipping out on her life. If only she understood why he ran off. Had she done something wrong to drive him away? She'd never been able to come up with anything. But now that they'd encountered each other again all these years later, Tyler had displayed neither guilt nor an inclination to explain. Unacceptable.

Equally unacceptable was lingering at her father's bedside when she should be doing her part to end the threat against him, not to mention the threat against herself. At least now, with a guard on duty, she could feel free to get on with the investigation. She might be able to bring herself to thank Tyler for that much thoughtfulness.

Movement in the hallway snagged Jen's attention. Dr. Ashraf hustled toward her. Jen stood aside to allow the doctor into her father's room. The woman began examining her patient while Jen hovered near the doorway, shifting her weight from foot to foot. Had she misread her father's slight movements? Was he really waking up?

The doc made small humming noises as she leaned over her patient, with her stethoscope alighting here and there on his chest. Then she stood up straight and faced Jen.

"Mr. Blackwell's condition is definitely improving. We will soon begin weaning him from the ventilator."

Jen's heart lightened and she smiled. "That's great news. Thank you, Doctor. Please have someone notify me when he wakes up. I need to get back to tracking down whoever attacked my father."

And me and Tyler, too. She kept those last words to herself even as thoughts of Arthur Gillespie's family learning of the death of their loved one sent a pang through her. This ruthless murderer had a lot to answer for.

Jen stepped into the hallway and came to a halt. A familiar figure in a park service uniform strode toward her.

Tyler offered a grim nod as he came up to

her. "I see the protection detail beat me here." He jerked his chin toward Red, who answered with a lift of a hand in greeting.

"Why are you back at the hospital?" Jen's tone came out sharper than she intended, but honestly, he needed to stick to the important business of catching a killer looking to strike again.

Tyler's eyes narrowed. "Are you telling me you *don't* need a ride back to the assisted living facility to get your car?"

"I told you I'd grab a rideshare."

He shook his head. "Not on your life when your life is literally being threatened."

His wordplay failed to spark a grin from her. "I don't need a bodyguard. I can take care of myself."

"You demonstrated as much in the parking lot against brute-zilla, but two of us working together is safer than one alone."

His admiring tone marginally soothed Jen's irritation. "Since you're here, anyway, I wouldn't mind a lift to pick up my vehicle. I need to run home and change out of my jogging outfit, then get to work on the case."

She fell into step with Tyler as they headed out of the hospital.

He glanced toward her, blue eyes probing.

"Want to hear what the parking lot attacker had to say for himself?"

They got on the elevator. "You interviewed him already?"

Tyler shrugged. "It wasn't much of an interview. The guy didn't know anything except he was paid to put you out of commission or at least 'distract you'."

"Distract me from what?"

They left the elevator and headed toward the front door.

"From whom, I think, is the better question. I believe the answer is to distract you from your father and his condition. Since your rush to his bedside at the assisted living facility and getting timely help for him stalled your father's death, our bright but diabolical adversary had to scramble to find a way to keep you from realizing your dad had to have been drugged—at least long enough for it to be too late to save him with the antidote."

Jen scowled as they stepped out of the hospital into the bright sunshine. "Mr. Adversary succeeded in his distraction. Of course, I was so frazzled that a distraction probably wasn't necessary. *You're* the one who had his head on straight and realized what must have happened. Thank you, by the way."

"You're most welcome. I'm parked over

here." He led the way across the lot, threading between vehicles.

Jen suppressed a shiver as the remembered image of a massive fist heading for her face passed across her mind's eye. "Who hired the guy to attack me?"

"He had no idea. The assignment came to him anonymously through a knock on his apartment door, which he opened to find an envelope with payment and instructions on his doormat. Apparently this pillar of society will do almost anything for a few bucks."

They climbed into Tyler's white with green trim park service pickup.

"Why don't you take me to my apartment and let me change clothes first?" She buckled the passenger seat belt. "Then you can run me over to my car, and I can zip on in from there to the department. The logistics of distance and direction make more sense that way."

"My pleasure." Tyler sent her the sort of companionable grin that used to set her heart tripping over itself.

Used to? She quickly looked away from him. The wattage hadn't dimmed, and neither had her reaction. *Get it together, girl.* The chance for anything between the two of them had long since passed. Best that she keep that knowledge in the forefront of her mind at all times.

In a subdued tone, Jen gave Tyler directions to her apartment in a modest yet well-kept neighborhood. Her complex was small, with only sixteen units, eight facing one direction and eight facing the other way in two stories of stacked units of four on a floor. There was nothing fancy about the building, but the management company kept it tidy. She put herself in Tyler's shoes as he observed the complex when they stopped in the parking lot, and she gave thanks that the grounds made an attractive first impression with the grass mowed and spring flowers blooming in beds along the sidewalk.

"Wait here." She shoved her door open. "I'll just be a min—"

She cut off her sentence with the cessation of engine noise and the soft creak of Tyler opening his door.

"I guess you're coming in."

"Walk you to your door at least."

He was still guarding her. Jen swallowed her scowl and barely managed not to stomp as she proceeded ahead of him toward her first-floor apartment. She would have preferred the second floor for security reasons, but nothing on the upper floor had been available. At least the small, cement patio adjoining the front entrance was screened by a white PVC privacy fence. Even if an intruder managed to unlock the gate, they'd be stopped by the dead bolt on the other side, leaving them with the option of a precarious scramble over the serrated fence-top to gain access to the large sliding glass door leading into her living room. Her front door was guarded by a high-end lock she'd installed herself with the owner's permission, as well as a video doorbell. A cop needed to be mindful of extra security.

"You might as well come in." She stabbed her key toward the lock.

"Stop!"

Tyler's sudden bellow froze Jen to the spot, and her heart leaped into her throat. The man stepped up behind her and pulled her to himself with one iron arm.

"What?" She started to resist.

"Stop." The softer hiss was more urgent than his shout.

He pointed toward her doorknob. Her eyes widened. A filament wire as thin as gossamer and nearly invisible wrapped the knob. Then he traced the line with his pointing finger up to the overhang of the walkway above. Her gaze followed his finger and came to rest on a claylike square object stuck to a wooden beam attached to the cement walkway overhead. A metal prong poked out of the clay with a small light blinking like an evil red eye at its tip.

A bomb. And opening her door would have set it off.

Jen had heard the expression about the blood freezing in a person's veins and had considered it a bit of hyperbole. She stood corrected now that the phenomenon had turned her to icy stone.

Struggling to take in a full breath, Tyler clutched Jen to himself. How easy it would have been to overlook the millisecond flash of sunlight on the filament wire long enough for her to open the door and set the bomb off, turning them both into hamburger. Without his military training, he wouldn't have realized what a wire like that signified or recognized the substance called C-4 that comprised the bulk of the compact explosive device.

"Let's back away slowly and then call the bomb squad." He spoke softly in Jen's ear. Not that the volume of his voice could detonate the C-4, but his throat was too tight to allow him to talk louder.

Jen offered a sharp nod but no words as an answer. He would have been surprised if she could say anything at all.

In shuffling lockstep, they backed away and

put distance between themselves and her front door. Then they broke apart, and Jen slumped against the side of his pickup truck. All the blood seemed to have drained from her face.

Tyler swiped his phone from his utility belt and called the Gatlinburg PD. A minute later he ended the call.

"They're getting the squad together."

Jen responded with a terse okay, and he studied his companion. Color had returned to her skin. She was standing straight now, her gaze fixed on her apartment building.

"What about my neighbors? We have to evacuate them."

"Who is likely to be home this time of day?"

"I've only lived here a few weeks, so I'm not well-acquainted with everyone." Jen's head turned this way and that, apparently scanning the nearly vacant parking lot. "We don't have designated spots, so I'm trying to match vehicles to renters by memory." She pointed toward a little white Camry. "I know one belongs to my next-door neighbor, a single mom with a couple of small children. She told me something about a settlement after her husband's accidental death that allows her to be at home with her kids."

"We should get them out of there for sure. Who lives above you and to the other side of you? Those are the most vulnerable units if the device blows up."

Her green eyes fixed on him. "How likely is the bomb to go off spontaneously?"

"Not very. As far as explosives go, C-4 is among the most stable."

Jen exhaled a long breath. "The guy above me works at a bank, and I don't see his car in the lot. The couple in the other unit beside me also work during the day, so their cars are gone."

"I'll go get mama and her kids."

"*We'll* do it. She knows me."

Tyler nodded acquiescence. He might have known Jen wouldn't delegate a potentially dangerous task. She hadn't lost an ounce of her innate guts and determination to do right that he'd so respected in her while they were growing up. The woman was the complete package—courageous, honest and beautiful. He was only now appreciating how desperately he'd missed her. Did she feel the same way?

A muscle in his jaw flexed as he followed her up the walk. What did it matter what either of them felt for the other? An irreparable gulf of withheld knowledge remained fixed between them. If he spoke up now, she'd hate him worse than she already did for ruining her relationship with her father in the time they had remaining to them before ALS took him from her.

A few minutes later, he and Jen were standing in the parking lot with the young family, awaiting the arrival of the bomb squad. The small children were restless and whiny, wanting to go back inside and play with their toys or have a snack.

"Maybe I should take them to the park and get them away from here," the young mother, an attractive brunette named Marsha, suggested in a faint tone. She gnawed her lower lip as she gazed apprehensively toward the front of their building.

"Not a bad idea," Tyler answered.

Jen turned toward the woman. "Did you see anyone approach my door after I left this morning?"

Marsha shrugged. "I looked out the window about nine thirty, when a UPS truck pulled into the lot. The guy who got out with a package had his hat pulled down. I didn't see his face, and then Mikey spilled his juice, so I had to deal with that and didn't pay any attention to what door the guy went to. Do you think he's the guy who booby-trapped your place?"

Tyler shook his head. "Hard to say. He could have been an innocent delivery driver."

A boxy truck with the GPD insignia on its

side pulled briskly into the apartment's parking lot.

"The bomb squad's here." Tyler lifted his hand toward the oncoming vehicle.

Jen touched her neighbor's arm. "Later, we'll want an official statement from you, but for now, you should go with your kids. The technicians won't want you here while they work."

The woman wasted no time buckling her children into their car seats and leaving the lot while the squad piled out of their vehicle and began donning their safety equipment.

Tyler approached the tall woman who, by her issuing of orders, appeared in charge of the bomb detail.

She turned toward him. "Did you call this in?"

"That was me, Tyler Cade, Department of the Interior law enforcement agent. We seem to have a small block of C-4 hooked up to a detonator wire attached to Detective Jennifer Blackwell's front doorknob."

"Sergeant Sandra O'Keefe, Gatlinburg PD." The woman introduced herself with an outstretched hand. "Good information on the bomb. How did you recognize all that?"

"Army training. Just enough to know what I was looking at. Not enough to feel comfortable attempting to neutralize the device."

"Smart to recognize one's limitations."

The woman offered a brief grin as her three full-suited squad members joined them in a small huddle. Jen's approach rounded out the group.

"Before your guys go in," Jen said, "let's check my video doorbell app to see if it was the UPS driver who placed my unwelcome gift. Maybe you'll get a clue that will help you defuse it."

"Good idea," O'Keefe answered.

The bomb squad knocked back their hoods for better viewing. Jen tapped at her screen as the group formed a semicircle around her.

"Majorly gutsy to plant a bomb in broad daylight, but it couldn't have been there when I left for my run in the park this morning."

"Or the timing of the bomb's placement may indicate desperation," Tyler put in.

Jen held her phone at arm's length as if she were attempting a selfie and thumbed the icon. "I've got it set to start the replay at nine twenty-five."

Silence fell as the video progressed, showing nothing but a dormant parking lot. Tyler had to hand it to Jen for investing in a high-end video unit because the picture quality was clear and sharp. Evidently, the recording was continuous rather than motion-activated. Another uptick in the price tag for video storage, but it made sense for a cop to keep a continuous eye on their environment.

Then, at around the nine twenty-seven mark, the familiar dark brown bulk of a UPS truck stopped almost directly in front of the camera's lens. A uniformed male emerged holding a rectangular parcel under one arm. Was the package big enough to contain the components of the bomb attached to Jen's door? Tyler estimated that it was.

The man strode confidently toward Jen's door, but his facial features were all but unidentifiable. A billed hat pulled low overshadowed his face. Dark sunglasses hid his eyes, and his mouth and chin were obscured behind thick facial hair. Tyler's muscles tensed. This level of feature obscurement hinted that this guy was likely their would-be bomber. The beard could even be artificial. The man stopped so close to Jen's door that his face was out of the picture, leaving only his shirt and a few buttons in view. A gloved hand flashed across the screen, and then the video went dark.

"What!" Jen's exclamation held both anger and frustration.

"He covered the lens." Tyler let out a frustrated grunt. "Probably with tape that he removed after the deed was done. The lens was clear when we arrived."

O'Keefe sighed. "We won't see anything related to his method of setting up the bomb. The way you described the device indicates a fairly straightforward configuration anyway, but we won't assume anything." She turned toward her people. "I don't think we'll need the full-court press on this one. Loggins—" she nodded toward one man "—head on in and take a look at what we've got, and then call for whoever or whatever you need to do the job."

Loggins acknowledged the order by pulling his hood over his face and waddling off toward Jen's front door. A hand wrapped around Tyler's arm, and he glanced over to find Jen standing beside him, her gaze riveted on the man moving in to disarm the bomb that had been intended to take her life.

"I hate this," she murmured without shifting her gaze from the bomb squad member. "I despise someone risking themselves for me."

Tyler placed his hand over the smaller one gripping his arm. "He's not risking himself for you. He's doing his job."

"I know, but people can still get hurt...or worse."

The skin on Tyler's arms prickled. The inflection in her words implied a meaning deeper than a general concern for others. He knew nothing about her life between the time he left Mount Airy and today, when they'd literally collided at the national park. Could the current threat to her life be connected to something from that time period and have nothing to do with the incident that sent him away from her? At least then there would be no need to dig up dark truths.

She might not like it, but he would have to pry into those missing years because the danger wouldn't let up for her or possibly others around her until a killer was in custody. Between now and then, he had to stick close to her and keep her safe. Her father, too, or else Tyler's long-ago sacrifice would mean nothing. Then, once she was safe, if Jen still despised him, he'd bow out of their lives for good.

If only he could find satisfaction in that decision. But the more time he spent in Jen's presence, the more he wondered if he'd made the right choice to leave his hometown and all he cared about behind fourteen years ago. Then again, what else could he have done?

SIX

"All clear." Loggins stepped up the sidewalk toward the group as lightly as his bulky suit allowed. In both arms, he cradled a box containing the dismantled components of the bomb. His craggy face glistened with sweat, but he wore a smile.

A muted cheer sounded. For the first time in most of an hour, Jen allowed herself a full breath. She glanced around. A pair of squad cars had arrived a while ago to set up a perimeter and block the entrance and exit to the parking lot. The uniforms had gone door-to-door in the complex ensuring everyone was out of the building. And now the handful of evacuated but curious residents ringing the taped barrier plus the official personnel and the whirl of squad car lights lent a certain bizarre, circus-like quality to the contained area. Not exactly the impression she wanted to make on her neighbors.

Jen let out a long sigh. "I still need to change clothes and report downtown."

A familiar van trundled up the street, and the uniforms pulled a squad car back to let it enter the lot.

"The crime scene techs are here," Tyler said. "They'll want to see if the bomber left any forensic evidence before they'll allow you to open your door."

A feline snarl erupted from Jen's throat. "I wish I could say this has been the worst day of my life, but it has certainly been among the most frustrating."

"And dangerous." Tyler sent her a sidelong look that implied the question of what day might have been worse than this.

"Probably tied for the honor."

He frowned. "You'll have to explain that statement if it could have any connection to what's currently going on."

"I don't see how that would be possible."

His stern stare remained upon her. She lifted her hands in surrender.

"All right. You want to know? Last year, my partner was killed in a shoot-out with a convenience store robber."

"In Memphis?" Tyler's gaze softened.

She nodded, her throat thickening against her will. "While the robbery was going on, the clerk tripped a hidden alarm. We happened to be less than a block away from the store when the call came in, so we got there in seconds. The thief was wired out of his gourd on meth. On our arrival, he burst out the door and escalated instantly to blasting away with his handgun. We returned fire from the squad car, and the suspect went down."

"Your partner took a bullet, too?"

She shook her head. "Not then. With our adrenaline through the roof, we exited our vehicle and approached the suspect cautiously, our guns trained on him. He wasn't moving, but that didn't mean the threat had ended. The guy was still breathing when we got close, but he appeared to be unconscious. I kicked his gun away, holstered my duty weapon, then knelt to see if I could slow the bleeding from his chest wound. Grant, my partner, got on his shoulder mic to call for an ambulance. Then a woman burst out the door of the convenience store screeching that we killed her brother. She aimed her gun at me, but Grant stepped into the line of fire. The woman started shooting, and he shot back. He staggered out of the way in the second it took me to pull my weapon and respond to the threat. The woman dropped like a stone, and her gun skittered away. I turned to see if my partner was all right and..." Her voice trailed away.

"He wasn't," Tyler finished for her.

Jen shook her head, gaze fixed on her toes. "Grant and the female suspect were dead. The coroner never determined if it was his bullet or mine that ended the woman's life. Both shots were potentially lethal. The male suspect lived, but he's sentenced to incarceration for the rest of his life."

"Not a candidate to be running around shooting arrows, administering drugs to elderly care patients or planting bombs."

"No." She still didn't meet his gaze.

"I'm sorry that happened to you." His tone was warm honey on a still-raw wound. It soothed and stung at the same time. "So that was the most dangerous and worst day of your life."

Jen pressed her lips together and didn't answer. She wasn't about to correct him on the worst day part. Sure, she was still dealing with a truckload of grief over losing her partner on top of the necessity of shooting a suspect. But that incident lacked the element of utter betrayal contained in the day she arrived home after a weeklong, post-graduation trip with girlfriends to Charlotte, North Carolina, to find a Realtor pounding down a For Sale sign next door in Tyler's yard. Her excitement to tell him all about the trip—the sightseeing, the concert they'd taken in—evaporated instantly. She'd marched over to find out what was going on. The Realtor had stared at her blankly for a moment, then told Jen her client had left town and expected to handle the sale remotely because he wasn't coming back.

And he hadn't.

Lava fizzed through Jen's veins, but she bottled the eruption of angry words behind a locked jaw and simply walked away from Tyler. His gaze burned on her retreating back. She felt the stare as tangibly as the sun on her head. But turning around was no more an option than opening her mouth to say anything. She needed a little space to get herself together. A day of reckoning was coming, but not today.

Jen walked up behind the crime scene crew, one of whom was print-dusting everything around her front door while the other one stood on a step stool examining the area where the C-4 had been planted, searching for trace evidence.

The one on the stool looked down at her and shook his head. "I don't think there's going to be anything to find. Maybe something will turn up when we look closely at the bomb components."

He got off the stool, folded it up and stuck it under his arm. "You about done, Mitch?"

The one doing the fingerprint dusting began putting his powder and brush away in his kit. "I pulled a few prints off the doorknob and one off the doorbell."

"Thanks, guys." Jen shook hands with them. "I'd be shocked if our suspect left any prints behind. The ones you collected from the knob will likely come back as mine, and if my neighbor, Marsha, will allow you to take her prints the one on the doorbell is probably hers."

"Right." The fingerprint technician nodded. "If your neighbor would stop in and give her prints that would be really helpful."

"I'll ask her. Now, may I go inside, please?"

"Have at it." The tech with the stool waved toward her door, then turned and headed back to their van with his partner following.

Jen's gaze followed them, and then Tyler began to make his way toward her, a determined set to his jaw. No doubt he felt it incumbent upon himself to check her apartment in case there had been an intruder.

"I'll be fine." Jen lifted a forestalling hand. "The bomb was planted *outside* the door. It's unlikely anyone went in. Besides, I'm well able to clear a space on my own."

Tyler stopped in front of her. "I believe you, but I'll wait here while you verify the environment is safe."

Jen gritted her teeth against a futile protest. Then, heart rate ramping up slightly, she used her key in the lock, turned the knob and stepped into her apartment. A familiar light scent of lavender potpourri greeted her, and all her furnishings stood in place. There was no sign or subliminal sense that an intruder had entered. She could be thankful for that small mercy. Still, she hadn't lived here long enough for the apartment to feel like home. The violation of her space—albeit her outdoor space—heightened the sense of otherness about her environment.

Maybe she should move. No, changing her address was no solution while someone out there seemed to be watching and setting traps for her. Hadn't that been at least partially what the scenario with her father's financial advisor had been all about? Ensuring she'd stop and check out the body, making her a stationary target. But why the bow and arrow gig? There had to be some sort of significance in that choice of weapon.

Questions dogged Jen's steps as she traveled smoothly and silently through each room, one hand on the butt of her weapon. At last, she returned to the living room.

"All clear!" She projected the words toward Tyler's shadowed figure waiting at the front threshold.

"Good news." He closed her door, and the faint tromp of his boots against the sidewalk faded away.

Inhaling a long breath, Jen went into the bathroom where she quickly washed up. No time for a full shower. Next, she changed into a business casual suit appropriate for a plain-clothes police detective and then turned her ponytail into a neat bun coiled at the nape of her neck. Finally, she ensured all her accoutrements, such as her badge and gun, were firmly in place.

About twenty minutes after she stepped through her front door, she was striding out of it again. She locked up, turned around and froze. All city law enforcement personnel had left the area, but Tyler remained, leaning against the front grill of his pickup, one knee bent, with the booted heel resting on the bumper and arms crossed over his chest like he had all day to lounge around.

That's right! Her car was still parked in the assisted living lot. She was dependent on Tyler for a ride. This day kept getting better and better.

At the sight of Jen in her dark suit befitting a police detective, Tyler bottled the words of admiration that sprang to his lips. The thunderclouds on her face clearly communicated that she wasn't currently open to compliments. At least, not from him.

He planted both feet on the ground and stood up straight. "Let's go grab some lunch and dissect this case. We haven't yet had a chance to slow down and think about what we've got so far."

"Lunch?" She consulted her watch, and her eyebrows climbed her forehead as she stepped toward him. "I can't believe it's that time already, and yet this entire morning has seemed to drag on forever." She stopped in front of him and lifted her gaze to his. "Eating isn't on the menu right now. I need to show up for work finally, and besides, I don't know if I could stomach anything."

"Lunch," Tyler pronounced like the last word on the subject. "We've been going for hours like hamsters on a wheel. A little downtime will help us think, and food will give our brains and bodies fuel to move forward with this investigation. Don't worry about reporting to the office. We've been working this entire time. Your captain understands that."

Jen opened her mouth, but then her gaze dropped and she shut her jaw with a sharp nod. "You're right. We need to slow down and take stock. Perpetual motion isn't necessarily a sign of progress. I don't know if I'll be able to swallow a bite, but a glass of water and a cup of coffee sounds fantastic."

Tyler went to the driver's-side door of his pickup and climbed inside. Jen joined him in the cab seconds later. They fastened their seat belts, and Tyler drove the truck out of the lot.

"This is a nice neighborhood." Jen gazed out her side window. "Not ritzy, but not broken down either. When I first moved in, my landlord and neighbors were thrilled to have a cop around, but now I wonder if they'll feel the same way."

"That's a legitimate concern, but once we catch this guy, your presence will return to being a tick in the plus column."

"Then let's get after this person."

"He's already locked up with no release date in sight. Only he doesn't know it yet."

Jen's gaze swiveled his way, and a smile flickered across her face. Tyler's pulse sped up. That smile used to fuel his life with inspiration. How he'd missed that look on her face, like they were sharing a joke that no one else got. He wanted to be a permanent fixture in her life again so badly his heart hurt.

Tyler cleared his throat and concentrated on his driving. "I know a place that serves the best burger and fries I've ever tasted, bar none."

"You know what? My mouth is watering. Maybe I'll be able to eat after all."

Ten minutes later, they parked outside a small mom-and-pop restaurant with an outer facade that could use a paint job. Tyler chuckled at Jen's questioning look.

"Don't let the exterior fool you, or the worn interior for that matter. Lilah's Diner is a mainstay in this neighborhood. They're not looking to attract the tourist crowd. Only locals know about it—and people like me who are good friends with a local. My boss, Lamont, lives with his family near here."

They got out and went inside, where Tyler led them to a corner booth away from the scattering of other patrons lingering over a late lunch. The appearance of a man in a National Park Services uniform and a woman with a badge clipped to her belt drew a few assessing stares, but people soon returned to minding their own business.

Jen slid into the booth across from him, her gaze scanning the room. "I'd put the decor on the shabby side of quaint, but the place is clean, and judging by the yummy odors—" she sniffed the air "—I'll trust you on the food quality."

A middle-aged server with a pleasant smile showed up with a pair of menus. Tyler waved his menu off, and Jen set hers on the table.

"I'd like a glass of water and a cup of coffee, black. Tyler here tells me you folks serve the best burgers and fries…like ever." She turned her eyes to his, challenging him.

He directed his attention to the server, whose smile had gone megawatt. "We'll each take a cheeseburger, medium-well, with fried onions and sides of fries. And I'll have what she's having for beverages."

"Comin' right up." The woman turned on her heels and marched away, scribbling on her order pad.

Tyler locked eyes with Jen. "Just like when…" His voice trailed away.

They used to order the same thing all the time at the local drive-in restaurant in Mount Airy. But this wasn't then and could never be again. Something like razor-sharp claws ripped through his insides. Their gazes separated. The fingers on Jen's hands resting on the tabletop twined together so tightly the knuckles whitened.

Tyler squared his shoulders. "We never did finish the conversation about who benefits if both you and your father passed away. Care to go over that with me?"

Jen's fingers disengaged from each other, and she sat back in her booth seat. "Okay. I already have an account that gets a percentage of the mine's profits, but I've never needed to touch the money. However, on Dad's passing, I get everything. Well, except for a few charitable bequests and a trust fund that's been set up and fully funded."

"Trust fund? For whom?"

"Dad's niece, my cousin Cinda, was born with severe Down syndrome. You never met her because she lives in Virginia."

"I think you've mentioned her to me."

"Right. Anyway, she's a few years older than me, and her mom passed away while I was in the police academy. Cinda needed to go into a care home, but it wasn't a very nice one because there wasn't much money for her care. So—"

"Let me guess. When the emerald mine was discovered, your father set up a trust fund to get her better care?"

"Spot-on. She's in a nice facility and has the best quality of life anyone could expect."

"Where's your cousin's father in all this?"

Jen shrugged. "He was never in the picture. Took off shortly after Cinda was born and didn't return or communicate." Her eyes narrowed on him to diamond-tipped lasers. No doubt comparing his disappearing behavior with the deadbeat dad's.

Tyler looked away, refusing to engage. He

was a better friend to her than she realized. "Do *you* have a will?"

"It would be foolish for me not to, especially given my high-risk occupation. But it's brief and to the point. The Blackwell gene pool has evaporated into a shallow puddle. With my dad's sister passing, that left only Cinda on his side. My mom was a Mayweather, but her gene pool was even shallower than ours. She *had* a messed-up brother, but he and one of his lowlife friends were killed years ago in an ill-conceived robbery at Harrah's Cherokee Casino."

A shiver went up Tyler's spine, but hopefully Jen didn't note the slight quake in his body. Her attention had moved toward the server who was placing steaming plates before them.

"Get you folks anything else?" She set a bottle of ketchup on the table.

"No. This looks fabulous." Jen smiled up at the server.

"I'm good," Tyler added.

"Enjoy." The woman whirled and headed toward the kitchen.

Silence fell for a season, except for soft hums of pleasure as the burgers and fries steadily disappeared. Most of the appreciative noises came from Jen. Tyler's appetite had abruptly waned, though he forced himself to finish the food he'd touted so highly. His companion couldn't be allowed to see that their conversation had gone in a direction that soured him.

At last, he shoved his empty plate away. "Are you telling me that Cinda's your sole heir as the last remaining blood relative?"

Jen wiped burger juice from her mouth. "Unless there are some obscure third or fourth cousins out there that we know nothing about."

Tyler furrowed his brow. "Who would handle the inheritance on Cinda's behalf?"

"The same board of directors that handles her trust fund."

"Who would inherit from Cinda?"

"The board would decide, but by then, what would I care?"

"Point taken." Tyler opened his mouth to continue the discussion, but the ringtone of Jen's cell began to sound.

She perked up and reached for her phone on her belt. "I hope it's the hospital to say Dad's awake." As she checked the screen, her whole body deflated. "It's Captain Mackey. Probably wondering where I am."

Jen answered the call in a brisk, professional tone. At first, there was "yes, sir," and then "no, sir," and finally "but, sir" as the color faded from her complexion. Tyler had an idea of what her captain was saying. He held out his hand toward her.

"Let me talk to him."

Jen blinked as if she'd suddenly remembered he was there. Tentatively, she offered her phone to him. *I don't want to be taken off this case,* she mouthed at him, confirming his assumption about what her captain was telling her.

"This is Tyler Cade, the federal park service agent in charge of investigating the murder committed on national park property. We've spoken before. I'm committed to working with your department on the related issues of the attempt on Jarod Blackwell's life and the attempts on Jen Blackwell's life."

The man on the other end of the connection grunted. "We can't assume the incidents are related."

"We can't assume they aren't. How big of a fan of coincidences are you?"

Silence fell. No cop cared for the idea of coincidence when a cluster of bad things happened involving the same set of persons.

"Do you have something else urgent you need to assign to Detective Blackwell?"

"Not urgent, but there are always things, and she shouldn't be involved in this specific investigation."

"Not normally, no, but I can't think of anyone more motivated to get to the bottom of events this morning, and she's already proven invaluable to my inquiries. In the spirit of a joint investigation, how about you leave her on the case teamed up with me?"

Something like a growl crossed with a splutter came from the other end. "Very well. She can act as a liaison between our department and yours. But Cade, you better keep my detective alive."

The gruff guy cared about his people. Good to know.

Tyler smiled even though Captain Mackey couldn't see his face. "My plan exactly. Any updates for me?"

"Just a few things. A pair of uniforms did the death notification to Arthur Gillespie's family this morning. The widow said everything was fine at home, and Arthur left the house to go to the office at his usual early hour of six thirty a.m. He liked to get to the office before anyone else."

"What with that bomb thing this morning, I haven't had a chance to interview anyone at Gillespie's office."

"Already done. The guy never made it in that morning."

"Figures with the timeline. He was hijacked by the killer somewhere between his house and his office. Is there any camera footage we could access between the two points?"

"I've got a unit on the hunt for that right now."

"You're on top of things. When Detective Blackwell's father wakes up, which could be any time, she'll want to rush to his bedside. She and I might as well do the interview with him at that time, and then I also have some inquiries in the works at the man's assisted living home."

The captain chuckled. "It seems as if we're covering each other's investigations, but since the events all appear connected, the arrangement is working. Put Detective Blackwell on again."

Tyler returned the phone to Jen, and the conversation wrapped up quickly with the captain delivering his updated information and presumably giving his detective her new orders.

Jen set the phone on the table and stared at Tyler. "Thank you."

The sentiment was correct, but something in the tone said she felt as if she'd sucked on a lemon. Tyler understood. Jen wanted—no, *needed*—to stay on the case, and if that meant she'd have to put up with being in his presence until it was over, she was willing to suffer, but she wasn't going to enjoy the proximity.

Her phone rang again, and Jen checked the screen. "It's the hospital this time."

She answered with a tense hello. Someone spoke on the other end, and her whole countenance brightened.

Jen ended the call and smiled at Tyler. "Dad's awake and breathing on his own. Well, except for his nasal cannula, but that's normal now. We need to see him. Maybe he can tell us who attacked him in his room at the care center."

Tyler attempted to smile back at her, but the burger in his stomach roiled. Acid bit at the back of his throat. Sure, in a professional sense, he needed to interview Jarod about the attack, but no, the last thing he cared to do was have a conversation with the man who had sent his life careening off track. His daughter's, too, but she'd never know why.

His stomach curdled. At least, he hoped she never would. How could he bear watching her heart shatter into a thousand pieces?

SEVEN

Jen's pace through the hospital hallways was little short of a jog. Tyler didn't seem to be keeping up, but she didn't care. She'd come close to having what time remained with her father cut short. Arriving at his room where his door stood open, she knocked on his doorframe to warn him he had a visitor, then stepped inside to find her dad sitting up with a meal tray before him on the overbed table. At her appearance, his face broke out in a wide grin, and he set his fork down on his plate.

"If it isn't…my baby girl." The last word was broken apart by a slight wheeze, but she'd grown used to the breathing impediment that often affected his speech.

"How are you feeling, Dad?" She came close and laid a hand on his bony shoulder.

"Right as rain. I hear… I have you to thank for reaching me in time."

"Not only me but—"

A sudden, harsh gasp from her father cut off her sentence. She turned in the direction of her dad's stare and found Tyler's athletic frame filling the doorway. Jen swiveled back toward her father. His face had gone pale as a sheet of paper.

"Dad! Are you all right?" She firmed her grip on his shoulder. "I know it's a shock, but Tyler is here to help. He's the one who realized you must have been drugged. And he saved my life today, too."

"Your life?" Slack-jawed, her father blinked at her. "What's going on?"

Jen could kick herself. She hadn't meant to blurt out anything about the danger to herself. They only needed to find out what her dad knew about the attack on him at the care center. But something within her had hastened to justify Tyler's presence and motivate her father to regard the prodigal favorably. Why would she react with an instinct to try to repair the relationship between her father and Tyler, when her own relationship with the guy hadn't even begun to mend?

She was no psychologist, but she suspected the reaction meant she still cared deeply for Tyler even when she was sure she hated him. *Conflicted* didn't encapsulate the mess. With a supreme act of will, Jen stuffed her emotions away into a locked compartment and put on her cop hat.

"I'll get into that stuff later, Dad." She pulled up a chair to her father's bedside and sat down. "Tyler and I are investigating the attempt on your life."

"Why is Tyler…investigating?" Her father's gaze shifted between herself and Tyler and back again. "His uniform says…he's a park service ranger."

"I'm also a law enforcement agent with the Department of the Interior." Tyler stepped to the opposite side of the bed from Jen. "To put matters in context, your financial advisor, Arthur Gillespie, was found in the Great Smoky Mountains National Park murdered this morning. Given the time frame, Jen and I believe his death must be connected to the attempt on your life. What we need from you is anything you can recall about the attack at the care center."

While her father sat with his mouth gaping open, absorbing the information, Jen shot Tyler a grateful look. He'd respected her wishes to keep the danger to her out of the picture for the moment. She'd explain it all to her father eventually, but they needed to feed him the shocking details in pieces he could digest without sending his pulse and respirations to dangerous levels.

Jen grabbed her dad's hand and tugged. His gaze fell to hers, and the astonishment faded from his face. "That's...a lot to take in."

"Tell us what you remember, Dad."

Her father shook his head. "Not much, I'm afraid. It was dark...in my room. I recall waking up from...a sound sleep and seeing a large shadow standing over me. Then I felt a prick in my arm. My nasal cannula was yanked away, the room...started to whirl and everything faded to black. The next thing I know, I woke up here. I'm sorry... I can't be more help." The last words were barely a whisper.

"You're doing fine, Mr. Blackwell."

At the formal address, her father winced, and Jen had to bite her lip against a harsh word for Tyler. She needed to remember that this was a witness interview, not a friendly chat. Even if all was well between the parties involved, a degree of formality was in order, and her father would simply have to understand. So would she.

"Could you tell if the attacker was male or female?" Tyler continued.

"Male, definitely." A faraway look crossed her father's face as if he were concentrating on the incident. "I could tell by his silhouette, and he was wearing scrubs. I think...he had on a pair of those gloves the nurses and aides use.

His fingers…brushed against my arm when he shot that substance into me, and they felt rubbery. Not like…regular skin, you know."

"That's a good detail, Dad."

Her father wrinkled his nose. "It still doesn't identify who the creeper was. But…" His sentence trailed away.

"But what?" Tyler leaned in closer.

"He seemed familiar, but I can't put my finger on why… I felt that way."

"Familiar as a worker from the assisted living facility?"

Her father scrunched his eyebrows together. "No, that wasn't it. I felt…like I knew him from somewhere else."

"From Mount Airy?" Jen squeezed her father's hand.

"No, not a local…from the old hometown. I just don't know." Frustration bled through her father's tone.

"Let's let your dad rest." Tyler stepped back. "I think our next stop needs to be the assisted living facility. The GPD should have interviewed day staff by now, but I don't expect much for results. I'd like to touch base with the charge nurse about contacting the night staff in their homes. We could work together conducting some interviews ourselves." Tyler gestured toward Jen.

"Sounds like a plan." She released her father's hand and gave it a pat. "I'll be back later."

The man nodded with a frown on his face. "Don't think you're going...to get out of telling me the rest of the story."

"Never crossed my mind."

Her father harrumphed.

She grinned down at him. "We've never been good at keeping secrets from each other."

If she didn't know better, she'd swear a shiver coursed through her father's frail body, and he looked away from her toward Tyler, who was already walking toward the door with a stiff-legged gait. He didn't turn around to meet her father's stare.

"Thank you, Tyler," her father called at his retreating back. "For everything. I wish..." Her father's voice faded away, and he slumped against his pillow, puffing slightly.

The weight of each syllable, the almost-desperation in the tone conveyed the impression that her father was thanking Tyler for more, or perhaps *other* than his part in averting this morning's catastrophe with the fentanyl. Jen scowled as she followed her temporary partner out of the room. Off and on over the years, the thought had crossed her mind that something happened between her dad and Tyler that had provided the impetus for her best friend and teenage love to pull up stakes and disappear without a word. She'd even asked her father point-blank once, but he'd played her question off as silly, and she'd never brought the matter up to him again. Maybe she should have been more persistent.

They reached Tyler's truck without another word between them. Jen waited until she had her seat belt buckled to turn toward him, glaring fiercely.

"Are you going to tell me what happened between you and my father fourteen years ago?"

"No." He started the truck.

"No? Just no? That's all you have to say?"

"It's not for me to tell." Lips pressed together in a thin line and staring fixedly out the windshield, he put the pickup in gear and guided the vehicle toward the street.

The breath froze in Jen's lungs. So something *had* happened, and her father and Tyler had conspired all these years to keep it from her. What could possibly be that awful? A big part of her never wanted to know the answer, but it wasn't in her nature to ignore what must be faced. She was going to have to insist on answers from her father. The thought didn't intimidate her. No, it terrified her.

Tyler's insides alternated between hot and cold as he guided the truck toward the assisted living home. What had Jarod Blackwell been thinking about by getting involved in that tragic foolishness all those years ago? Hot. How was Jen going to feel when she found out? Cold. Tyler had sacrificed everything to keep her from knowing, and now it looked like the revelation was inevitable. Had been since they'd encountered one another out of the blue in the forest this morning.

God, what are You doing? Is this really for the best?

Tyler jerked his scrambling thoughts up short. He had no time for wallowing in a mire of old wounds and regrets. Someone out there was doing his level best to exterminate the two people he cared about the most in this life. There it was. The truth about how he felt toward Jen and Jarod Blackwell. Of course, he'd never stopped loving Jen. He had done what he had for that love. And yes, as much as he'd tried to deny it to himself all these years, he still loved Jarod like a father. Even what the guy had done didn't erase all those early years of looking up to him and learning from him. Once the killer was in custody, there would be a boatload of soul-baring to come. How it would all play out he had no idea. He'd best park the issue with Jesus for the time being.

They arrived at Silver Meadows Assisted

Living Home, and he slotted his pickup into one of the few vacant spots in the nearly full parking area. He put his hand on the door latch, but his phone dinged with a text message, so he held off on climbing out. Jen sent him a questioning look.

He pulled out his phone, checked the message and smiled. "The lab has some results for us. They are posting the results to the case file on the GPD network."

"We'll go to my desk at work and look those up after we're done here."

"Agreed."

They piled out and went into the building. The place was busier than when Tyler was here the last time. The residents were awake and out and about, and more staff was in evidence on the premises. Tyler led the way to the charge nurse's office. Decker was there, but he was standing up, and it looked like he was heading out.

Tyler blocked the doorway. "Did any of your aides or nursing staff report seeing a stranger on the floor last night?"

The charge nurse's cheeks reddened. "You'll have to take the issue up with administration. That's what they told me to tell you. The administrative offices are up the hall and to the right. If you'll excuse me, I've got to get to the shift change report meeting."

Jen barged past Tyler, practically knocking him over, and marched up to the nurse. Tyler stifled a laugh at Decker's quick backpedaling.

"This is an attempted murder investigation." Jen's sharp tone could have sliced boot leather. "We won't tolerate *any* obstruction. If you know something, you tell it."

The guy spread his hands in a placating gesture. "There was someone. Okay? But that's all I can tell you. No one will obstruct an investigation where one of our residents was endangered. They've got the information for you in the admin office."

Jen's stiff shoulders relaxed. "Thank you. I appreciate you doing your job, and I've always been pleased with the care my father receives here."

Decker perked up with a smile. "Glad to hear it. Sorry, my choice of words sounded like we might be giving you the runaround. If *my* dad was involved, I'd be in our faces, too."

"Thanks for understanding." Jen extended her hand, and the pair shook.

"How is Jarod? When will he be coming back?"

"He's recovering well, but I don't know the answer to your second question. That will be up to Dr. Ashraf at the hospital."

Decker smiled. "He's in good hands with Dr. Ashraf."

Tyler cleared his throat. "We've all got places to be. Thank you for your help, Decker."

"My pleasure."

Tyler backed out of the room, followed by Jen. They headed toward the administration offices, while Decker escaped in the opposite direction. An appropriately labeled door led into an area in the corner of the building brightly lit by sunlight streaming through large picture windows set at right angles.

The receptionist greeted them pleasantly and ushered them in to see the chief executive officer over the various Silver Meadows elder care campuses in the state. The nameplate on the desk said Renae Marlowe. The slender, gray-haired woman rose and shook their hands, but she wasn't smiling.

"How is Mr. Blackwell?" Marlowe asked as they all seated themselves in her spacious and tidy office.

Jen updated her as she had done for the charge nurse.

The CEO shook her head. "Terrible thing to happen."

Tyler sat forward. "What have you got for us?"

"Right to the point. I can tell you get things done, Mr. Cade."

"Tyler is fine, but yes, we like to move quickly in these sorts of investigations."

"I can hardly blame you." She lifted a manila folder from her desk and handed it to him. "There isn't much to go on. As Decker discovered, someone got into our computer system and wiped a video segment from Mr. Blackwell's hallway. They also deleted the records of a temp service aide who started work last night. We don't usually keep paper copies of such things unless they are requested. Storage issues, you know." She wrinkled her nose. "But quite by accident, my assistant printed the face sheet with the employee's basic info when she intended to print something else. She threw her error away, but we rescued the piece of paper from the shred pile, and it's in there. No photo, I'm afraid, and I'm suspicious that none of the information will hold up under scrutiny. We are dealing with the temp agency over the matter, but not your problem."

"Thank you for your diligence," Jen put in. "When we interview staff on duty last night, they should be able to give us a description of the person. Could we have a list of those people and their contact information?"

"Also in the packet. Most of them will still be sleeping. That's the way of it with the night staff."

"Understandable." Tyler rose, and the others did the same. "Thank you for your help."

"Of course." The woman nodded. "Let me know if there's anything else we can do."

"Count on it." Jen stood up.

Out in the hallway, she nudged Tyler with an elbow. "I can hardly wait to look at that employee face sheet. Bogus information or not, it's something to sink our teeth into."

"We'll do it in the pickup."

"No way." She shook her head. "I'm going to drive out of here in my own car."

They reached the front door and stepped outside into the warm sunshine tempered by a pleasant breeze that played with tendrils of her hair that had escaped from her professional bun. Tyler willed himself not to notice the soft strands reaching forward to caress her face. Years ago—and yet it seemed like yesterday— he would have brushed the locks away and kissed her. Any such attempt today would receive the same welcome as the assailant in the hospital parking lot.

He forced himself to turn away from her and scan the area. "Where *is* your vehicle?"

"My little red Mazda's over here." She led the way past several vehicles in a row near the front of the building, then stopped short with a sharp hiss.

Tyler nearly piled into her. "What's the matter?"

"Look."

He stepped around her and spied a vehicle sitting lower than it should be because all the tires were slashed open like someone had gone wild with a machete. A deep groan escaped him. What purpose would someone have to slice her tires?

"This is just petty." Jen's tone dripped scorn.

From a small grove on a distant hill, a flash of something metal glinting in the sun caught the corner of Tyler's eye. His heart seized. Or maybe there *was* a purpose. He lunged for Jen, and they tumbled toward the asphalt. In that split second, a shot rang out.

EIGHT

As they hit the asphalt, Tyler on top of her, the breath gushed from Jen's lungs. The back of her head bounced against the pavement, her hair bun slightly cushioning the blow. Still, her senses spun as the passenger-side rearview mirror sprayed apart above them into jagged shrapnel that pinged off surrounding objects. Tyler's body sheltered most of hers, and he let out a pained grunt. Some shrapnel must have hit him.

Jen's adrenaline spiked through the roof, and oxygen flooded her chest. She shoved Tyler off her, scrambled to her knees and grabbed his arm.

"Let's get to cover."

She half dragged and half guided Tyler to a spot in front of a neighboring vehicle that would put them out of the shooter's sight and an impenetrable engine block between them and the long-range weapon. That is if she had correctly calculated the direction the bullet must have originated.

"I'm okay." Tyler pulled his arm from her convulsive grip.

"No, you're not. You have a shard of metal sticking out of your upper back."

Jen frowned at the bloodstain spreading slowly across his shirt from the site. Other smaller spots also dotted the fabric, betraying further strikes by small chunks of glass or the metal framing of the mirror, any of which might be embedded beneath the skin.

"The least of our worries." Tyler drew his gun. "I don't know how our pistols will fare going up against a rifle."

"Exactly." Jen drew her phone and called for help.

"I'm sure they've already called 911 from inside the facility."

"What a nightmare for the staff and residents." She grimaced and glanced over her shoulder toward the assisted living building. "How did you know we were under threat?"

"Suspicious glint of sunlight on metal from a woodsy hill where there shouldn't be anything reflective. The dude could be waiting for one of us to pop out of cover." Tyler risked a glimpse over the hood of the vehicle they were crouched behind.

Jen yanked him back down. "Don't play the mole inviting a whack. Let's wait for the cavalry."

"But he's going to get away."

"Little doubt he's already gone. You drew no response from your whack-a-mole imitation."

Tyler's taut posture eased, and he let out a hiss. "*Now* I'm feeling that shrapnel in my back. Can you remove it?"

"Not a chance, Tyger. I'm going to let the EMTs pull it out. I have no idea how deep the wound goes and what might be damaged in there."

He scoffed. "There's not enough material in that side mirror for a shard to be very long."

"Nevertheless." She gave him a look and enjoyed the satisfaction of him shutting his mouth with only a mild scowl. Stubborn always had been Tyler's middle name. "Thanks." She reached out and gripped his hand.

"For what?"

"For knocking me out of the way of a bullet, for one thing." She smirked at him. "And for the bruises I'm going to have on my back, not to mention the near-concussion and for just about cracking my ribs when you landed on me. Thanks to you, I'm almost fine."

Tyler started laughing, then stopped abruptly

with a grimace. "I hope the emergency services get here shortly."

No sooner had the words left his mouth when sirens began to close in on their location. Minutes later, the parking lot flooded with police cars followed by an ambulance. Then a SWAT van pulled up in the near distance and disgorged a team in full gear that rapidly surrounded the hillock where the sniper had taken his shot. The team began to close the perimeter, and Jen lost sight of them in the trees.

A pair of EMTs began ushering Tyler toward the ambulance, and Jen followed in their wake, keeping her sense alert for any gunfire coming from the area of the sniper's perch. The continued quiet from that direction was both reassuring and dismaying. There would be no shoot-out, but she'd probably been right to believe the shooter had gotten away. It would come as a pleasant surprise if the SWAT team emerged with the suspect in tow.

"We'll have to take you to the hospital and have a doctor remove the shrapnel," said an EMT to Tyler, "and check you out for further embedded objects."

Tyler stopped walking, nearly tripping up everyone in his vicinity. "I don't think anything is embedded very deeply. Can't you just fix me up and let me go?"

"No, sir."

"We have to decline."

"Don't be an idiot."

The chorus of denials came from the male EMT, the female EMT and Jen, in that order. Tyler huffed and allowed himself to be guided to a waiting gurney. Brisk movement drew Jen's attention, and she turned her head to find her lean, gray-haired captain striding toward her, wearing a red-faced scowl. Her stomach sank.

"We're going to have to put you in protective custody." The man halted in front of her. "Enough is enough."

Jen opened her mouth then closed it again. She'd brought danger to a care home for the elderly and to her neighbors at her apartment complex. Apparently there was a target on her back the size of the moon. Now Tyler was injured. Her captain was right. Enough was enough. But tucking tail and hiding seemed counterproductive.

"You trust your fellow cops, don't you?" Captain Mackey seemed to have read her thoughts. "Let them get to the bottom of this without putting more citizens at risk. We want to keep *you* safe, too."

Jen's insides went hollow. "But my dad—"

"Is under protection at the hospital."

"But—"

The loud clearing of a throat brought both their heads around. Jen frowned down at Tyler, who had deigned to settle facedown on the gurney. However, one arm dangled off the side with a fist gripping a wheel brake, not allowing the longsuffering EMTs to take him to the ambulance's rear. The effort was costing him some pain as evidenced by the whiteness around his lips.

The aggravating man ignored Jen but fixed a sober stare at her superior. "I agree with you that Detective Blackwell needs to be somewhere away from the public and yet safe for her. Would you say the department headquarters would fit the bill…at least for the rest of today?"

A rapid gamut of expressions contorted the captain's expression—a deep scowl, followed by wide-eyed thoughtfulness and then a smooth smile. "She would indeed be safe at the department and away from innocent civilians. But—" a milder form of the scowl returned "—I still have my reservations about her continuing on this case."

"I don't share those reservations." Tyler lifted his head higher with a grimace. "Right before the sniper attack, we received a call about evidence results. I'd like her to follow up on those for me from the safety of her desk."

Heat rolled ominously through Jen. "Tyler, I don't need you negotiating for me."

"But *I* need you to stay on top of the case's progress while I'm receiving medical attention."

Captain Mackey chuckled, and Jen fought back the fire in her cheeks that flirted with spontaneous combustion.

"Which would you prefer, Detective?" her boss asked. "Desk duty or watching game shows at a cushy safe house?"

Jen banked her ire. *Later, Tyger.* She smiled, smooth as butter, at her captain. "Show me to my desk, sir. I've got work to do."

"Come with me. I'll take you there myself."

"Yes, sir." Jen turned toward Tyler. "And stop being a jerk to the EMTs. They've got a job to do, too."

"Yes, Detective." Tyler released the hand brake.

Jen turned on her heel and followed her boss toward his vehicle.

"I'll join you at police headquarters as soon as possible."

Tyler's voice followed her, but she didn't bother to turn around or answer. Why did that man so easily get on her last nerve? And why did her gut clench at the thought of him having that shard of metal removed from his back? She was no doctor, but the shrapnel's location appeared dangerously close to his heart.

Jen sent up a prayer for Tyler and to give the doctors wisdom as she joined Captain Mackey in his unmarked car. During the drive to the headquarters building, she ran through all that had happened since her traumatic discovery of the financial advisor's body until the attack at the care center. Some of the information Mackey had heard about already. Some of the details were new to him. The man asked a few incisive questions, and then they arrived at their destination.

The captain pulled to a stop and double-parked outside the front of the building. He left the engine idling. "Go on in and find your desk in the detective area of the bullpen. One of our IT people will get you going on your PC. I've got a meeting to attend with the mayor and the chief of police."

Tightness cinched Jen's chest. "Is the get-together about what's going on with me?"

"I imagine the subject will come up, but this meeting was already set before today. Thank you for the update. Now I'll have a better idea of what to tell the higher-ups."

Her tension eased, but only marginally.

"Thank you for the ride and for the support of the department."

The captain smiled, deepening the lines at the edges of his smoke gray eyes. "Law enforcement folks have to stand together. Go. Be safe."

Jen got out of the car and hurried into the building. The public waiting area was the usual daytime hive of activity in city police departments, with civilians coming and going on various matters and police personnel hustling by. The dispatcher behind his bulletproof window was prepared for her arrival with a keycard for the inner reaches of the building and an ID lanyard. Jen wasted no time pushing through the restricted entrance and heading for the desk she'd been assigned on the second floor at the time of her orientation.

When she entered the bullpen, a generous smattering of desks was filled with cops doing paperwork or pursuing leads online. A few of them acknowledged her when she went past, but most kept their heads buried in their computer screens. Jen had no problem flying under the radar. The last thing she needed was a bunch of questions or commiseration. She reached her far corner spot, the normal, out-of-the-way location for a newbie, and sank into her chair.

A sense of disembodied detachment filled her, and she gripped the edge of her desk with white-knuckled fingers. She should have been sitting here since early this morning, not only just now in the middle of the afternoon, finding her place. All the harrowing events and the horrible images flowed over her in a wave. She struggled to breathe, and blackness edged her vision.

Dimly she registered a lanky figure approaching her desk carrying a small box. The twentysomething guy stopped in front of her. Jen gulped in oxygen and forced herself to focus.

"Are you the IT person who's supposed to get me set up in the department computer network?"

"That's me." The guy smiled. "Derek Slen at your service. I even brought you a desk-warming gift."

Jen's gaze zeroed in on the open, unwrapped box. Suddenly, all keyboard clatter and conversation ceased. Jen scanned the room. Every eye was upon her. She gulped.

"A gift?" Her voice came out strained.

"What every cop must have daily." Derek retrieved two items from his box and set them before her with the air of a server at a high-end restaurant.

Jen blinked at the chipped, stained mug and the crumbling confection on a torn napkin.

The IT guy's smile turned into a full-blown grin. "Burned coffee and a stale doughnut."

The entire room erupted into laughter. A dam released inside of Jen, and she joined them in hilarity until she wiped tears from her eyes. How she loved department camaraderie. This was her welcome razzing. Now she felt right at home.

Please, God, let this be my lasting workplace.

Her prayer could only come true if they caught the creep targeting her and her family. And yet, that priority seemed to take a back seat in her psyche to whatever might be happening with Tyler at this very moment. What did that say about her true feelings toward the man who had once broken her heart into tiny pieces? The question didn't bear thinking about.

"Mr. Cade, the shard of metal entered your back in a location near the heart." The emergency room doctor stood over Tyler. "I'd like you to lie as still as possible until we get the ultrasound results evaluated. When I know the shrapnel's exact position, I should be able to remove it safely."

"Understood." Tyler stifled a groan.

The doctor stepped out of the room, and Tyler was left alone with his thoughts. He'd had better company.

Besides being wheeled to another area for the ultrasound, he'd been lying in this exam room for over an hour. The pain had intensified by the minute. He didn't need the doc to tell him twice to lie still. And yet, inside he was keyed up like a spring ready to bust loose. Urgent questions chased themselves through his mind. Was Jen safely at her desk? What had she found out from the evidence techs? Would the results help them solve the case? And the prize question of all: who wanted Jen and her father dead and why? If they found the who, he had no doubt they'd know the why, or vice versa. They simply needed a nudge in the right direction.

At last the doc returned, and the nurse behind him, wheeling a cart bearing a variety of instruments.

"Good news," Dr. Philips said heartily. "I believe we can pull the metal straight out without a surgical procedure to avoid nicking the heart."

The nurse approached, bearing a syringe. "I'm going to numb the area around the shrapnel. The lack of sensation will allow you to remain perfectly still when Dr. Philips removes the foreign object."

Cade grunted his assent. The entrance of the needle stung slightly but soon all sensation faded from a large section of his back. He didn't miss the pain. A faint bitter odor and light pressure on the injured area signaled the nurse swabbing around the shrapnel with disinfectant. Then the doctor picked up forceps and leaned over Tyler. A painless pinch followed, and the doc stood back, eyeing the sharp metal triangle gripped in the forceps.

"Gotcha!" The doctor's tone held a triumphal note. "You can be thankful, Mr. Cade. If this shard had been a few millimeters longer, you would have been stabbed in the heart, and we would be having an entirely different encounter involving emergency surgery. Or perhaps, we might not even have had time to get that far."

A shiver ran through Tyler. "Trust me. I'm very thankful."

The nurse swabbed the injury further while the doctor placed the blood-slicked metal onto a tray and picked up a needle already threaded with sutures.

"Now we'll patch you up." Dr. Philips got to work.

Forty-five minutes later, Tyler was discharged

and walked out of the ER sporting several stitches and numerous small adhesive bandages on his back where smaller bits of shrapnel had invaded his flesh and been excised. None of the minor cuts required stitches, but they stung worse than the larger injury. Of course, that circumstance would no doubt change when the anesthetic wore off.

The rideshare he'd called was waiting for him outside the door, and he eased himself into the back seat. First, he'd retrieve his pickup from the assisted living parking lot then head on to GPD headquarters. Anticipation as much as any discomfort from the wound on his back kept Tyler on the edge of his seat in the car.

As they pulled in, the care center parking lot appeared entirely normal, but Tyler noted glass and debris around the spot where Jen's car had sat. The vehicle itself had been hauled away and was probably in the police evidence lot by now. As he got out of the car, a pair of uniformed maintenance technicians emerged from the care center and headed with brooms toward the mess. Clean-up time.

Tyler's truck, not being part of the crime scene, sat where he'd left it. He quickly retrieved the go-bag he kept in the rear compartment that held, among other things, a spare park ranger uniform. He changed his blood-stained shirt and then got into the driver's seat. The folder of information from the care center administrator sat in the seat next to him. He and Jen would need to follow up on any potential leads contained inside. Tyler started the vehicle and headed toward GPD headquarters.

His urge to see Jen again bordered on compulsion and not solely because she was in danger. He'd forgotten how much he enjoyed—no, craved her company. Before he'd left Mount Airy, her companionship had been as necessary to his well-being as food and drink. The cost to him of leaving her behind had been almost more than he could bear.

At last he found a parking place near the GPD and managed to get through the rigmarole admitting him to the inner parts of the building. He climbed the stairs to the second floor, nodding to several passing officers who sent him curious looks. Arriving in the squad room, he gazed around, landing on and dismissing various heads behind desks, until at last Jen's sleek blond hair grabbed his attention. She hadn't noticed him because her gaze was transfixed on whatever appeared on her computer screen.

Tyler headed in her direction and almost reached her workstation when her head swiveled toward him. Her distracted expression morphed into a brilliant smile that was abruptly swallowed by aloof sobriety. Tyler's heart did a little jig. She was happy to see him, but not ready to show it because she was still angry with him. And with cause, he had to admit. But the problem wasn't something he could fix in a moment, if ever. Either way, her reaction betrayed that she still cared.

Jen stood up from her chair. "You're all right. Good. What did the doctor say?"

"I narrowly avoided being stabbed in the heart, but it turned out to be a minor wound after all. I've got a few stitches and will be sore for a while. Small potatoes compared to what could have happened. How are your bruises?"

She shrugged. "Similar small potatoes. What isn't small are the results the evidence technicians and the coroner have produced."

"Show me."

He deposited the folder he carried onto the desktop for future attention. Then he snagged a stray chair and pulled it up beside Jen's. They both sat down, and Jen angled her computer screen so they could read the contents together.

"This is the preliminary coroner's report on Arthur Gillespie. Look at this bit." She highlighted a paragraph. "Our concept of this case just got turned upside down."

Tyler leaned closer and took in the words. Then he sat back with his jaw agape.

"I know. Right?" Jen turned a bemused gaze on him.

"Did I read that correctly? Mr. Gillespie was dead *before* the arrow struck his body?"

"That's what the coroner concluded. And he was not killed at the park."

"What about the scream you heard before you came upon the body?"

"Obviously it wasn't Arthur's shriek."

"The killer's cry?"

"I can't think of anyone else who could have made the sound. The scene was a setup—a piece of elaborate theater."

"Directed entirely at you."

"Apparently."

Tyler gently gnawed the inside of his cheek as he ran over the crime scene in his head and stopped on one glaring detail. "I should have noticed."

"Noticed what?"

"Gillespie's shiny shoes."

"His what?"

He met Jen's puzzled gaze. "If Gillespie hiked up that trail on his own two feet, there's no way his shoes would have remained pristine. Someone transported his dead body."

"One of those four-wheelers your department uses would do the trick."

"We didn't see such a vehicle in the area. Nor did we hear an engine start when the suspect escaped. No, the guy drove Gillespie's car to the base of the trail then toted the body over his shoulder like a deer carcass to his selected spot."

"Of course!" Jen smacked her hands together. "He set up the scene exactly how he wanted it, complete with an arrow in the body's chest, and lay in wait for me."

"I'd say that's correct, but it's also disturbing on many levels."

"You're telling me!" Jen snorted and slumped in her chair, face pale.

"To hike two miles up that trail carrying significant weight indicates someone physically strong with superior stamina."

"Not to mention a twisted and cunning mind."

"Agreed. As well as a wide variety of skills."

"Right. He's not only a muscle man and a competent archer but also a bomber and a sniper."

"What sort of person is capable in all those areas?"

Jen shot him a lopsided smile. "Um, some sort of super-soldier."

Tyler pursed his lips and nodded slowly. "Makes sense."

Jen barked a laugh. "I was kidding."

"I'm not. This guy probably has military background."

"*That* I can grant, but even specifying the likelihood this killer has military training, the suspect pool remains enormous."

"The number can be whittled considerably if we only include individuals with that background who are connected to you and/or your father."

"That's the thing." Jen spread her hands, palms up. "Other than a colleague or two from the Memphis PD, I can't think of a single family member or close acquaintance meeting that criteria."

"Could the killer be hired muscle like the guy who attacked you in the hospital parking lot?"

"Do you think a hireling would put on that elaborate charade on the hiking trail? The scenario feels entirely too personal and vindictive."

Tyler sighed. "I hate to agree with you, but I do." He wasn't sure which emotion took precedence—disappointment or frustration. Nothing about this case seemed simple or straightforward. "Let's move on for the moment from this avenue of inquiry. Maybe the suspicion that this guy has military training will connect with another piece of evidence down the road. You said something was interesting in the CSI report."

Jen blanched so that the slight dusting of pale freckles across her nose that he'd always found so charming stood out. Turning away from him, she clicked a new tab on her screen, and a different report came up.

Tyler scanned the screen because she didn't seem inclined to point anything out. The report contained initial findings from the piece of paper containing the threatening note retrieved from under her car's windshield at the national park. His gaze stopped at a certain item, and he sucked in a breath.

"What were your father's fingerprints doing on the paper?"

NINE

Heat replaced the chill that had momentarily gripped Jen in an icy fist. This guy was playing mind games with her and her father even as he tried to kill them. Who of their acquaintances could possibly think so diabolically? Jen couldn't come up with a soul. But what stranger would have the motive?

She met Tyler's expectant gaze. "As you know, Dad was in the military during the Persian Gulf conflict in the 1980s, so it's no mystery why his prints were in the system decades later to be matched with the print on the sheet of paper found on my car. The big problem comes in the fact that, to my knowledge, my father has no copy paper in his room at the care center."

"Could the fake nursing assistant have brought the sheet of paper with him and put your dad's fingerprints on it after rendering him unconscious?"

Jen rolled her shoulders in a shrug. "Why do that when he had no reason to anticipate needing to leave a note for me? He thought he was simply going to kill me."

Tyler nodded. "I can see that reasoning. Then where did the paper come from?"

A shiver ran through Jen. "The only other place this creep could have gotten paper my father handled is our family home in Mount Airy."

Tyler's brow furrowed as he met her gaze. "Do you still own the house?"

"Yes, but I haven't been back there since Dad moved into the care center. The house is locked up tight with a security system engaged, and a caretaker stops by periodically to check on the property. We have no plans to sell. At least, not at this time."

"Could you call the caretaker and see if there's been a break-in?"

Jen frowned. "I can do that, but if the alarm had gone off or if someone had left signs of unlawful entry that the caretaker spotted, we would have been notified."

"Maybe someone got past the security system, and the incident is too recent to have been discovered yet by the caretaker."

A tremor ran through Jen from top to toe. "For some reason, despite all the dangerous attacks we've suffered, the idea of a malicious stranger violating the privacy of our home seems the creepiest of all."

"I've heard that's a common reaction from people whose homes have been broken into. Still, there's no proof yet that it happened."

"Other than the mysterious sheet of copy paper with my dad's prints on it that couldn't have come from anywhere else." The wheels of her rolling chair gave a slight rumble as she pushed backward. "I need a cup of coffee before I make the call."

"What's this, then?" He waved toward the stained mug on her desktop.

She chuckled. "The cup of brown sludge and the crumbling doughnut next to it are desk-warming gifts from my new brothers and sisters of the GPD."

Tyler grinned. "I see they wasted no time in officially welcoming you. Are you sure they won't be offended if you go get a different cup of joe?"

"Not if I leave their token of affection in prominent display at least until the end of shift. Want to join me in the break room?"

Tyler waved her off. "I'm going to call my station and see how things are going. Maybe something suspicious has been spotted since I've been away, but I'm not holding my breath because no one's been blowing up my phone to report anything. Actually, my phone probably *will* blow up with Lamont's yells when he finds out the scrapes you and I have gotten into since we left this morning."

"Sounds about right. Can I bring you a cup?"

"Cop-shop coffee crossing this refined palate? Are you serious?"

Jen snorted. "Ri-i-ight, Mr. Army Ranger. I'm sure you've never been exposed to anything except high-end java served by a professional barista."

"You've got me there." He raised his hands. "If it's not too much trouble, you can bring me a mug, too. We've got more evidence to go over, and I think our brains are going to need all the stimulation they can get."

"Coming right up."

Chuckling, Jen turned on her heel and walked away. From the easy banter they shared, one would think their camaraderie had never been interrupted. But the relationship *had* been disrupted, and she still didn't know why. A scowl replaced her smile. She needed to remember that while she and Tyler were necessary allies in this case, they weren't friends anymore and probably never would be again.

When she returned to her desk with two cups

of coffee, Jen had her professional mask firmly in place.

"Hope you like it black." She set the mug in front of him.

He picked it up and took a sniff at the rising steam. "Is there any other way?"

"Sure. My way with a healthy dollop of cream and half a packet of sweetener. *Un*-healthy but delicious. My big indulgence."

Since she said her piece without a hint of levity, Tyler seemed to get the hint that the casual banter was over. He returned his attention to the computer screen.

"Anything new in the reports or from your people out at the national park?"

"All quiet at the park—or as quiet as it gets at the beginning of the busy season. But why don't you put in your call to Mount Airy and then we'll look at the reports together?"

Standing beside her desk, Jen pulled her cell phone from its holder on her belt. Why was she so reluctant to find out if her childhood home had suffered an invasion? Maybe because the sense of home and belonging had been so integral to her childhood and teenage life. Not everyone could say that, and she dreaded having hers become tainted in any way. Nevertheless, she didn't flinch as the call went through and she asked David Lang the caretaker to have a look at the property. She ended the call and set her phone down.

"David will get back to me after he's had a chance to go over there."

His gaze fixed on the computer screen, Tyler nodded distractedly.

"What do you see?" Jen settled into her chair and pulled herself closer to the computer.

"The coroner has completed the autopsy on Mr. Gillespie. Shortly before he died, he suffered several bruising blows to his abdomen and torso."

"Someone beat him?"

"It looks that way."

"Ah!" Tyler pointed to a line item. "Here's the actual COD, and it isn't an arrow to the chest or blunt force trauma."

Jen's eyes widened at the listed cause of death. "A heart attack? Dad's financial advisor passed away of natural causes?"

"Not necessarily. The blood toxicology report hasn't come back from the lab yet. It's possible some sort of poison caused the heart attack. Our guy used fentanyl on your father."

"Granted, but it says here that Gillespie's overall physical condition, including severe hypertension, as well as partially blocked arteries discovered during the autopsy would have made him a prime candidate for his heart to give out."

"True enough." Tyler sat back against his chair and then jerked upright again with a hiss.

"Pain?" She scanned his stiffened torso and tightened lips.

"I guess the anesthetic has worn off."

"Maybe you should go home and get some rest."

Jen got no response to the suggestion as Tyler's eyes swiveled back and forth across the autopsy report. She joined him in reading.

"Nothing else unusual," he said at last.

"I concur, but the heart attack death doesn't mean our assailant isn't a killer."

"His becoming a murderer is not for lack of trying, with multiple counts of attempted homicide."

Jen let out a low hum and narrowed her gaze at the report. "What if this large-muscled, ruthless individual wanted something from Arthur Gillespie, and a combination of the beating and the intimidation frightened the guy into a fatal heart attack?"

"My thought exactly. Which *does* add up to indictable murder."

"Though a little harder to convict."

"Which still leaves the question of what this crook thought to gain by interrogating your father's financial advisor."

Jen opened her mouth to speculate, but her

ringtone halted the thought. "It's the caretaker in Mount Airy." She answered the call and listened, her heart wringing in her chest.

When the conversation ended, she sat frozen in her seat, her cell phone held in limbo between her ear and the desk.

"What is it?" Tyler gently prompted, his voice reaching her as if from a distance.

Jen swallowed and pulled in the breath she'd been forgetting to take. "Someone destroyed the security system—including disengaging the emergency notification function that the system has failed. And they proceeded to trash our place from one end to the other." Her voice came to a raspy halt.

Tyler grabbed her hand, but Jen yanked it away and surged to her feet. "I've got to go to Mount Airy."

Tyler rose slowly with his hands extended in a placating gesture. While he understood her reaction, he had to stop Jen from taking an impulsive and dangerous action.

"You can't go anywhere. Think about your father."

"I *am* thinking of him." Her volume rose to a near shout. "This will devastate him. I've got to fix it."

The room went silent, Jen's cry grabbing attention like a bullhorn. Tyler didn't turn around to see for himself, but he had no doubt every eye was fastened on their drama. Jen's cheeks reddened, and she let out a soft huff as she sank back into her chair.

"I'm sorry." She refused to look at him as he resumed his seat beside her. "Of course I can't leave town with Dad in the hospital and both of us under threat."

The hum of voices in the room picked up where it left off, but Tyler leaned toward her anyway to aid the confidentiality of their conversation.

"I get your frustration. I'm sickened by all that's going on."

"We have to get to the bottom of it."

"We will."

"I don't… I just…" She pressed two fingers against each side of her skull and rubbed. "I feel like my head will explode if one more stupid thing happens. Trashing our house is petty and malicious, but it doesn't compare with trying to kill us. Yet I'm as upset about that as anything else."

"I suspect the home invasion happened before the attempts on your lives began. Maybe he grabbed some paper to make notes for himself. The plotting behind these attacks is elaborate enough to require it."

Jen stopped rubbing her temples, took in a deep breath and let it out slowly. "Okay, I'm rational again. What's our next move?" Her determined gaze captured his.

"We should get crime scene techs into your family home to hunt for evidence left by the intruder. They won't be able to tell if anything's missing, but they might be able to determine how he gained access, and they could look for evidence, such as fingerprints, or maybe he cut himself during the destruction."

"You don't have to convince me." She offered a faint smile. "I'll call the police chief in Mount Airy. He's a family friend. He'll make the arrangements."

Tyler nodded. "Do that. Then let's continue checking reports and following leads. Something has to spark a connection that will lead us to what is going on and who is behind these attacks."

"I appreciate your confidence." Jen's frown held a hint of despair as she grabbed her phone and placed the call.

While she spoke with the Mount Airy police chief, Tyler gritted his teeth. If he weren't careful, anger would get the best of him, and *he'd* be making rash decisions. In their youth, he was always the cool head to Jen's fierce and good-hearted reflex to plunge in and right wrongs. Since then, military training had reinforced in him the value of tactics. Still, at times he had to admit, Jen's instinctive response in certain situations *had* been the perfect tactic. Growing up together, they'd found their natures providing checks and balances to each other that had worked well.

Involuntarily, a soft chuckle left his lips. Jen ended her call and turned toward him.

"What are you laughing about?"

"Sorry. My mind got off track. Do you remember the time in fifth grade when Brady Perkins was running a protection racket on the playground?"

Jen's eyes sparked. "Any kid he deemed wimpy had to pay him something from their lunch box, or he or one of his two minions, Elliot Tracy or Randy Givens, would pop them in the face."

"When you discovered why so many bloody noses were happening on the playground, you wanted to run right over and kick that bully in the shin."

"A noble endeavor, but one that might easily have ended with me getting jumped by Elliot and Randy and my own nose bloodied. You grabbed my arm and stopped me and told me we needed a plan to take them out all at once."

"Some elaborate plan it was." Tyler snorted.

"It's a wonder we weren't caught and hauled into the principal's office. Where would the justice have been in that outcome?"

"The simultaneous, two-pronged attack worked, didn't it?" Jen giggled. "And none among the grateful horde of victims would rat us out."

"When Brady's greedy mitts were full of ill-gotten foodstuffs, you swooped in and kicked *both* his shins."

"While you strode over and popped the minions' noses—left, right—just like that."

They grinned at each other.

"Hah!" Tyler sipped at his coffee as the memory played through his head. "Brady hobbled around for a week afterward."

"And Elliot and Randy hustled the other direction whenever they saw you."

"I wonder whatever happened to Brady. I remember his family had moved away by the next school year."

"I can answer that question."

"Really?"

"He moved back to Mount Airy about a decade ago to open an auto body shop."

Tyler's eyes widened. "I hope he's not causing problems."

"Not at all. The adult Brady is a really nice

guy, a solid family man and an asset to the community."

"Wow! Maybe a couple of sore shins did the dude a world of good."

"Too bad bloody-nose therapy didn't fix whatever was wrong in Elliot's and Randy's attitudes." Jen scowled and shook her head. "Elliot continues to live in Mount Airy and is a hard-drinking loafer who's driven away two wives. And last I knew Randy joined the Navy, got dishonorably discharged and later went to prison for armed robbery. Then again, he didn't have any kind of decent fatherly example. His dad was killed along with my mother's brother, Ansel, trying to rob a casino the day after we all graduated high school. Wonderful graduation present for him." Her expression hardened, and she abruptly returned her attention to the computer screen.

Tyler's heart battered his rib cage, and his wound throbbed. His departure from their hometown happened during the same time frame, and Jen was dangerously close to connecting the dots. *He* hadn't done anything wrong—at least, not any more than he'd had to do. But he'd rather have her think that of him than realize the truth.

Of course, the longer this investigation went on, the greater the chance that buried secrets would be unearthed. In the face of Jen's dogged determination to know what had driven Tyler away, that consequence might be inevitable. The situation was like watching an impending train wreck and not being able to do anything to stop it. Maybe the best he could manage would be to keep Jen and her father safe from the attacks of this outside third party.

Then again—a chill coursed through Tyler—maybe the would-be killer was *not* an outsider to buried history. Maybe he *was* connected to that long-ago tragic mess and was not after Jen and Jarod for their emerald mine. According to Jen, it sure didn't seem like there was an obvious suspect set to inherit among the remnants of their family tree. If greed were eliminated as the motive, then revenge for past sins might come into play. But who among the living, other than Jarod and himself, would know what had happened?

Maybe Jen had given him a clue in her casual anecdote—Randy Givens, who'd lost his father in that idiotic casino heist. Tyler didn't understand how Freemont Givens's son would know the details of what went on fourteen years ago unless Freemont had told him the plan before it happened. But then, why wait this long to do anything about it? Randy could have spoken up right away. Or not. Certain types of families raised their children to mistrust and avoid law enforcement at all costs. The Givens bunch fit the demographic. No, Randy would be the sort hardwired to handle his problems extra-legally, possibly even violently.

Tyler shook his head, unable to get out of his own private thoughts to concentrate on the crime scene reports that kept Jen riveted. Or maybe her thoughts were all over the place, too, and she was pretending to focus the same way he was doing.

At some point, without Jen knowing, he needed to inquire if Randy was still in prison. If the man remained behind bars, Tyler could gladly abandon suspicion in that direction. The fact that the Blackwells' financial advisor was a piece of the puzzle tended to swing the likely motive back toward the greed angle. But if Randy Givens were free, the revenge motive would have to be investigated. A lot more digging into the past would be necessary, regardless of the consequences to the relationship between Jen, her father, and himself. The fallout would be hideous, but better than death.

Maybe.

TEN

What was bugging Tyler? Despite the gravity of the situation, he'd been Mr. Cool Cucumber until she'd explained what became of the larcenous Randy Givens and his lowlife father, Freemont. Could whatever sent Tyler away from Mount Airy so abruptly and mysteriously have something to do with the Givenses? Tyler hadn't been sucked into something illegal with them, had he?

Jen mentally shook her head. No, stealing didn't fit Tyler's character either then or now. If only he would simply tell her the truth. After all the heartache he'd caused her, didn't he owe her that much? Evidently, he didn't think so, because he had yet to offer her a scrap of insight into what had been going through his head the day long ago when he'd left everything and everyone he knew in his dust.

Jen hazarded a sidelong look at Tyler, who

was pecking away at his phone sending a co-worker a text. Was he communicating with the lovely Rachel? Making a date maybe? Her gut twisted. Jealous much? No! She'd convinced herself long ago that she was over Tyler, and she was going to stick with her convictions.

Tyler lowered his phone and pulled a sheet of paper out of the folder he'd brought in with him—the one from the assisted living administrator.

"This is the list of night staff at your dad's care center. The employees should be awake by now and able to take our calls and do interviews over the phone."

"In person is so much better."

"Agreed, but your captain has you on desk duty for the foreseeable future."

"Yes, but *you're* not chained to a desk."

He met her gaze. "I'll tell you what. It's likely that most of these chats are going to yield little useful information. Let's get started by phone, and if anybody seems to have important intel, I'll go interview them in person."

"Sounds like a plan." She plucked the list from his hand. "Let me make a second copy of this list. You can have one, and I'll have one, and we'll split the calls down the middle."

"Solid idea."

Jen headed for the copy machine that sat

in the opposite corner from her desk. As she walked, she greeted PD employees she'd met during her orientation. They responded in kind, but their speculative gazes followed her as she made her way to the machine. Everyone would be chafing to know who was trying to take out one of their own. *Not as much as me, GPD pals.* She made her copy and hurried back to her desk to find Tyler ending a call with a grim twist on his mouth.

"What?" She handed him his still-warm copy.

He raised a dismissive hand. "Let's get these interviews done, and then we'll see if any information we gather ties in with the fact that Randall Givens was released from state prison two weeks ago."

"Givens again." She scoffed. "What? You think he's getting back at me for helping thwart his protection racket in the fifth grade? If that were the case, I would think you'd be in the crosshairs, too."

"I was. Remember? I'd be a pincushion if you hadn't knocked me out of the way of that arrow in the woods."

"But it was me this killer tried to blow up—whether it's Randy or not."

"However, there's no way to know whether it was you or me he intended to take out with the sniper rifle. Possibly both of us."

"Granted, but those facts don't explain why you think it might have been Randy loosing the bowstring, setting the detonator and pulling the trigger. Or why he'd go after my father."

Tyler sighed as if the weight of the world sat on his chest. "The history over which Givens might bear a grudge is old but more recent than grade school. And now that we know he's on the loose, we'll have to look at the revenge motive."

Jen plopped into her chair and fixed him with a glare. "What history? And don't put me off again. I know this has to do with why you left Mount Airy. The time for secrets is over if it ever was called for in the first place."

"You'll have to make your own judgment call as to the necessity, but I made a promise I won't lightly break. I'll let you talk to your father first, but if you don't get your answers from him, you'll get them from me."

Their gazes locked. Jen breath came rapidly like she was fresh from a run, while Tyler's mouth tightened into a thin line rimmed with white. A steel trap if she'd ever seen one.

"Fine," she snapped out. "Let's get these interviews over with. By then, my shift should be over, and then I *am* going to talk to my father. In fact, I'll stay in his room overnight.

The police guard at the door should keep us both safe."

"Sounds like a sensible plan."

"And don't you sit outside the hospital like a mother hen."

Tyler let out a brief chuckle. "You mean like a warring eagle, don't you?"

She snorted. "Whatever image preserves your dignity. Go home tonight and get some rest. We need to be fresh to continue the investigation tomorrow."

"How fresh are you going to be after sleeping at the hospital?"

"Let me worry about that. I'm sure I can talk the staff into sparing me a cot. Now let's get these interviews started."

They divided up the list, and Tyler went to the small conference room to conduct his interviews while Jen stayed at her desk. The end of the workday dragged on forever. If only she could keep her mind on the repetitive questions she asked the potential witnesses and their equally repetitive and unenlightening answers.

Scant details of the mysterious temp aide emerged from her conversations with the night staff. Most of them had paid little attention to the guy who kept to himself and appeared to be doing his job in his assigned wing. Thus far, with typically conflicting witness statements, the guy could be anywhere from petite to average height. The discrepancy might be dependent on the height perspective of the witness. Some said the guy's hair was black; others said brown. Jen tentatively assumed the man's hair was in the brunette range.

At least everyone agreed the mystery aide was a little husky and wore oversized glasses that made his gray or green or hazel eyes appear owlish under their magnification, and he had a full face and a thick but neatly trimmed beard. The glasses and the beard could be camouflage, and contact lenses could change eye color, so those details were far from helpful. However, the few staff members who had spoken with him said he mumbled. Jen tapped her note-taking pen against her bottom lip. A mumbly voice? Maybe the guy had stuffed his cheeks with something to change the shape of his face.

Finally, Jen reached the last employee on her list, Maddie Tremaine. She began with the standard introduction of herself and the case she was inquiring about. The woman asked to be called by her first name, rather than Ms. Tremaine, and agreed to speak with Jen. Then she led off with a small but significant bombshell of information—she had been teamed up with the new aide on Jarod Blackwell's wing.

Jen's slumped shoulders straightened. "How much interaction did you have with the man?"

"Not as much as I usually have with a team-mate," Maddie said. "The guy kept to himself but did his work competently enough. He never asked me for help with anything. But it's night duty, which is less intensive in activities involving the residents and more tedious with routine chores like ensuring supplies are stocked for the morning, doing bed checks on our more dependent patients, charting and answering call lights."

"Understood. But working on the same station, I assume you got a good look at him."

"Sure, sure." The woman described an out-of-shape male with owlish glasses, dark hair, a close-cropped but thick beard, who might have a speech impediment. "Also, I know he was five feet, eight inches tall."

"How can you be so precise?"

Maddie snorted. "I'm all of five-eight myself. The temp guy and I were on the same level. We could look each other straight in the eye."

"Could heel height on either of your shoes have made a difference?"

"We both wore standard nursing shoes. That means plenty of padding and support, but not much of a heel."

"This is excellent information, Maddie. You've eliminated a suspect for us."

The woman laughed. "Great! Glad I could be of service. I hope you get this guy real soon."

"We're on it. It's possible we'll want you to testify. Would you be okay with that?"

"No problem."

Jen ended the call, laid her phone on the desk and sat back in her chair. Tall, lanky Randy Givens was no longer a viable suspect. She knew what he looked like, firsthand, and his characteristics were documented in his police file. People could disguise many things about themselves, and Jen surmised this guy had done so with his facial features and possibly with his body type by padding his clothing, but a six-foot-tall person could not cut themselves down to five-eight.

How should she feel about Randy being eliminated as a suspect? On the one hand, they now had no viable identified suspects. On the other hand, Tyler's theory that today's danger tied in with yesteryear's mysterious transgression was debunked, and whatever he and her father had gotten caught up in was not part of the current equation. She didn't know enough about that blot on the past to judge if that was a good thing or a bad thing.

Stirrings in the room indicated an impending shift change. Jen stood up and stretched her arms and shoulders just as Tyler came back into the bullpen. His frustrated expression told her he hadn't gotten much from his interviews.

"It's not Randy," she said as soon as he came within earshot. Then she explained how she had arrived at her determination.

Tyler looked anything but overjoyed. He opened his mouth to speak, but a uniformed officer hustled up to Jen's desk bearing a white, letter-sized envelope.

The guy extended the envelope toward her. "This was delivered for you downstairs, marked urgent."

Jen turned her head and met Tyler's narrow-eyed stare. He shook his head infinitesimally and reached for the envelope. Jen snatched it first but made no move to open it.

Tyler scowled then turned his attention toward the officer. "What did the delivery person look like?"

The officer shrugged. "One of the usual couriers from the local service—blonde, petite, cute but wearing a wedding ring. Too bad!" He grinned.

"Someone known to you, then." Jen gripped the envelope like it might escape from her.

"Most definitely."

"Okay. Thanks." Jen plopped into her seat,

examining the delivery front and back. "Nothing on this except my name and the word *urgent*." She raised the envelope toward the overhead light fixture. "Looks like a folded piece of paper and—oh no! There's powder in here."

She flung the envelope on her desk, recollected reports swirling through her head of ricin delivered in the mail to celebrities and politicians. Tyler's arms came around her, pulling her away from the potentially toxic object.

"We need the biohazard team in here!" he bellowed. "Now!"

Tyler stuck close to Jen as the squad room was evacuated. The small herd gravitated toward the large conference room on the third floor. Tyler didn't like the sidelong looks sent toward Jen from a few of her colleagues, as if she was toxic herself. After about ten minutes of milling around, Captain Mackey stepped into the room, his mouth set in a grim line.

He raised his arms for quiet, and the room settled. "The envelope has been safely collected by our biohazard team and taken away for analysis. Results will be shared when they come in, but for now, the workplace has been rendered safe for those of you coming on shift. For those of you ending your shifts, go on home. See you tomorrow."

A minor stampede headed for the exit, but Mackey gestured for Jen and Tyler to remain behind. When everyone else had left the room, the captain closed the door and turned toward them.

"I hate to say it, Detective Blackwell, but until this situation is resolved, it's best if you don't return to the building or even attempt to do police work. We really need to get you into protective custody."

Tyler opened his mouth to speak, but Jen preempted him.

"Already in place." She crossed her arms and lifted her chin. "I'll be spending the night in my father's hospital room with the police guard standing outside."

Mackey nodded. "Good enough for tonight. We'll figure something else out tomorrow. I can have a pair of uniforms drop you off at the hospital."

"Not necessary," Tyler spoke up. "I'll drive her there."

"Thanks." Jen offered a grim-faced nod. "We can swing through Bob's Barbecue and pick up something to go. I'm sure Dad would prefer a brisket sandwich to hospital food for supper."

"You got it." He forced a smile.

"That's settled, then." Mackey's lined face smoothed in some semblance of relief. "Be safe. I'll talk to you in the morning." The man strode out of the room.

Jen and Tyler made their way downstairs and left the building. Stepping outside into the almost-sultry late afternoon air, they both kept their heads on a swivel all the way to his pickup. Yet Tyler doubted the attacker would be interested in lurking around police headquarters, much less trying something in person there. After introducing a potentially toxic substance into the building through a third party, he'd be wise to make himself scarce. They followed her plan of picking up supper, though Tyler ordered nothing. The very idea of eating curdled his stomach.

Would Jen confront her father? Almost certainly. Would Jarod tell her what she stubbornly insisted on knowing? Maybe. But releasing long-held secrets didn't come easily.

"I'll walk you inside," he said as they turned into the hospital parking lot.

"Don't." Her tone was adamant. "Drop me off under the canopy in front of the door. I'll be fine."

Compressing his lips against a protest, Tyler pulled up where she indicated. He kept his gaze busy sweeping the area for threats. Just now, meeting her stern gaze was more than he could do. He blinked against sudden moisture in his eyes.

"Go home." Her tone came out harsh, and she cleared her throat. "Sorry. Go home, please, Tyler. This *has* to happen. Deal with it."

"Yes, Jen, I suppose it does." His tone came out thick, and he bowed his head.

She shut the door, turned on her heel and disappeared inside the hospital. Inhaling an uneven breath, Tyler put the truck in gear and headed out of the lot to drive the twenty minutes or so to his rural residence. His dog and her pups would be glad to see him, even if the woman who meant the most to him in all the world might never feel that way again.

It was already later than usual when he arrived home, and the remnants of his evening passed with excruciating slowness. Every minute moved forward like walking on broken glass. He tried to distract himself from the conversation that must be happening between Jen and her father by tending to household chores like throwing in a load of laundry. Normally, he enjoyed his modest log cabin located on several acres of forested land skirting the edge of the federal park. Chopping wood for his fireplace usually gave him great pleasure. Not tonight. The sense of satisfaction he gained from caring for his bluetick coonhound, Dixie, and her puppies was noticeably absent. Things must really be bad in his psyche if playing with five fuzzy, floppy-eared balls of cuteness and energy didn't keep his mind occupied.

At last, Tyler headed off to bed and lay awake with his eyes staring into the blackness. Could he have done things differently fourteen years ago? Sure, other choices were available—all of which ended in devastation for Jarod and, by extension, his daughter. *Should* he have done things differently was probably the better question. Possibly, because what he'd regarded as a self-sacrificial act had only postponed the devastation he'd hoped to head off entirely. Encountering Jen unexpectedly that morning had ensured the heartbreak.

Or *was* their encounter truly accidental?

Tyler sat bolt upright in bed with his breath frozen in his lungs. Had their mysterious adversary set him and Jennifer up to meet at that specific place and time? He and Jen had already intuited that the killer must have known her daily habits in order to plant the body of Arthur Gillespie exactly where she would find it. But was this vindictive jokester also aware of the route of Tyler's early morning rounds in the woods not far from his homestead? If so,

Jen hadn't been the only one under surveillance by hostile eyes taking in their schedules and habits.

Tyler's mouth went dry. Was *he* also a purposeful target of this ruthless criminal? If so, he was back to his conviction that the motive behind the deadly attacks was vengeance, not greed. But now, with Randy Givens eliminated as a suspect, Tyler returned to the question of who else besides himself and Jarod Blackwell could possibly know what transpired. He flopped back onto his pillow. No one, that's who.

His mind a messy stew of regrets, conjectures and dreads, Tyler drifted at last into a fitful slumber. The dream came, clearer than ever, but in the sped-up and jerky black-and-white of ancient cinematography.

Bam! Bam! Bam! The repeated hammering on Tyler's front door yanked him out of a sound sleep. He sat up in bed, blinking. The silvered moonlight that crept into his room through the edges of the blinds illuminated the shadows of familiar things. Growing up in this house under the care of his frail grandmother, he'd never known another bedroom to call his own. This was home.

The urgent knocking on his front door continued, and Tyler's heart began to hammer in rhythm with the noise. He was alone in the house. His faithful grandma had passed away only weeks ago of a heart attack, narrowly missing the milestone of his high school graduation that had meant so much to her—a milestone he'd reached today. He glanced over at the digital readout on his bedside clock. Or not today, but yesterday. The numerals said 3:07.

Who could be pounding on his door at this hour? Only one way to find out.

Tyler sat up and swiveled his feet onto the floor. The rag rug his grandma had handmade was soft against his soles. Sighing, he grabbed a T-shirt from the back of his desk chair and shrugged it on over his bare torso. The pajama bottoms he regularly wore to bed would make him presentable.

The staccato knocking suddenly ceased. Silence fell. The sound vacuum crowded against him like the walls were closing in. He stepped off the rug onto the cool hardwood of the bare floor, hurried into the hallway and then down the steps. The familiar creaks on the old stair boards should have been comforting, but instead, the sense of being trapped in a horror film came over him, slowing his progress.

Don't. Open. The. Door.

The words pounded in his brain like the hammer of fists that had echoed through the house moments ago. He was eighteen—had been for six months now—and a grown man, but little-boy fear snaked through him. Yet, as in the way of horror films, he was helpless to stop himself from reaching for the doorknob, turning it and pulling the portal open to find...

What?

No one was there.

No, wait. A figure slumped unmoving on his stoop.

"Mr. Blackwell? Jarod?" His next-door neighbor and father of the love of his life had invited Tyler to address him by his first name on Tyler's eighteenth birthday, but Tyler had yet to get used to that change marking a rite of passage.

Tyler squatted down by the crumpled form. The man's breathing was raspy and rapid. Tyler pressed his fingers to Jarod's wrist and found a jerky pulse. What was wrong? Then the moon came out from behind a cloud, illuminating wetness on Jarod's shoulder and all down his arm. Unlike reality, in the dream world, Tyler didn't have to investigate to realize the sticky substance was blood.

What should he do? His first impulse was to run and get Jen, but Jen wasn't home. She'd headed out right after the graduation ceremony for a week of fun and sun with girlfriends in Charlotte. The rare trip was a graduation gift from her father. To Tyler, her absence had ached like a sore tooth the minute she climbed into her friend's car and waved goodbye. But he'd see her again soon. What did a week of separation matter when they were going to be together for the rest of their lives?

No, Tyler needed to get emergency services here as soon as possible. He started to rise, but a hand gripped his arm, and Jarod Blackwell lifted his head.

"No cops. No ambulance." Jarod's whispered words were faint but adamant.

The stipulations from the wounded man made no sense, but at least the absence of liquor smell on his breath was a positive change. Jarod Blackwell had been using alcohol to self-medicate his grief over his wife's death from cancer three years ago. Some days, Tyler had to restrain himself from smacking the guy to remind him that others, like his daughter, were also hurting over that great loss. Because of the bottle Jarod climbed into, Jen had virtually lost both parents. Tyler, too, had lost both a mother and a father figure who had filled in relationship gaps his grandmother couldn't.

"Help me inside." The grip on Tyler's arm strengthened. "It's not a bad wound. You can treat it. I've lost a lot of blood, but I'll be okay."

"What happened?"

Jarod's only answer was a deep groan as Tyler helped the man to his feet and supported him to a seat in the kitchen. Tyler grabbed scissors and cut the bloody shirt away from Jarod's shoulder to reveal—

"That's a bullet wound!" His exclamation echoed in Tyler's dream ears as if he'd bellowed inside a hollow drum.

The nightmare slip-shifted past a chunk of time and resumed with Tyler seated across the table from the pale and shaking Jarod Blackwell, whose arm and shoulder were thickly bandaged in stark white. Did Tyler's subconscious shrink at reliving the gore and wrenching difficulty of removing the bullet, cleaning up the blood and applying the bandages? The question floated like a wispy cloud past his present-day self who lurked like an oddly aware yet not consciously awake onlooker to the tragedy. He knew he was dreaming but couldn't stop the dream from reaching its inevitable conclusion.

Jarod's tearstained cheeks glistened beneath the glow of the overhead lights. "We thought we were so smart, but we were just three drunks hunched over a sticky table in a smelly bar coming up with a half-baked plan to take down a well-guarded casino."

The image disappeared and segued to another.

Jarod's face rested on Tyler's kitchen table, buried in the crook of his uninjured arm. "Stupid, so stupid! We thought, 'Why not take ill-gotten gains and use them to support hardworking citizens?' Now Ansel and Freemont are dead."

The image dissolved and reformed into something different.

Jarod's eyes, fierce and determined, glared at him. "I was the getaway driver, but Freemont and Ansel were gunned down before they reached the car. I caught a stray bullet, but no one saw me. They don't know I was there. You can never tell Jen."

...never tell Jen...

...never tell Jen...

The three words reverberated in Tyler's ears as he jerked fully awake to the sound of his phone's ringtone. Dawn's earliest glimmer crept into his room through the edges of his curtains. He snatched up his phone and checked the caller ID. Jen.

"He-ello?" His voice quaked. What would she say to him—think of him—now?

"Dad finally confessed in the wee hours." Her tone was dead flat. "What right did either of you have to keep the truth from me all these years?"

"It wasn't like that. We were protecting you."

"Look how that turned out."

Her bitterness lashed at Tyler, and he cringed.

"Why did protecting me mean you had to leave?" Deep hurt bled through her tone.

"I promised your father I wouldn't tell you. And I promised myself, too. I couldn't bear to ruin your relationship with your remaining parent. But I knew if I stayed, I couldn't face you every day and keep the secret safe. I thought—" Tyler struggled to speak through a thickened throat. "I thought the only way you'd never know was if I gave you up."

Silence fell for several heartbeats.

"You know he never drank a drop afterward. He became the best father I could ever want. Even better than before Mom died."

"That's a good thing, right?" His stuttering heart rate began to even out. Maybe things would be okay.

"A good thing? Maybe *then* it was. But now, understanding the context? The death? The blood? The years of secrecy? I don't know if I can forgive either of you."

Tyler's insides froze. That was his everything's-black-and-white Jen talking. Exactly as he'd feared.

"What are you going to do?"

"Go away."

"What? A killer is after you and your father." *Me, too, I think.* He stopped himself from verbalizing the suspicion that had occurred to him last night. He had no corroboration. Yet.

"Nobody will know where I've gone. I'll be fine. I'm trusting you to look after Dad. You've done it before. Better than me, apparently. I always wondered why Dad's shoulder seemed to hurt him for a while after I returned from Charlotte. He insisted he'd fallen off a ladder but would be fine. Some joke, huh?"

"Are you still at the hospital?"

"Not for long."

Tyler hopped out of bed, grabbing one-handed for his clothes. "Stay there. I'm on my way. We can talk this out."

"Goodbye, Tyler. I can take care of myself. Don't follow me."

The connection ended. Stomach roiling, Tyler pulled the cell phone away from his ear and stared at the silent instrument. He had to stop Jen from leaving, or failing that, he had to find her. Yes, her life was in danger, and that was reason enough to want to keep her close. But even more, he was done being without her. He'd run *away* from her once. This time, he was going to run *to* her.

ELEVEN

Jen swiped tears from her cheeks for what seemed like the hundredth time since she'd left the hospital and rented a car. Driving with filmed vision wasn't ideal, but nothing inside her allowed letting up on the gas pedal until she arrived at her destination. At least she had the presence of mind to keep an eye out for anyone who might be following her. So far, she'd spotted no suspicious vehicle on her tail.

How could her daddy—the man who'd kissed her boo-boos when she was little and cheered her on in track when she was older—have gotten mixed up in some harebrained scheme to rob a casino? Sure, money had been tight back then, and at the time, he'd been pickling himself in the bottle for several years and not in his right mind. But even so, she would never in a thousand years have guessed her father had a larcenous bone in his body.

A picture of him last night, gazing at her

from his hospital bed with huge, sad eyes, flashed in her mind. "But baby girl," he'd said, "in my muddled brain I'd convinced myself I was doing it for you. Then you could pay for college and not need to scramble for scholarships, take out student loans or work yourself to the bone while you tried to study."

So now it was *her* fault he'd gotten himself mixed up in something that ended with his brother-in-law, Ansel, and the man's ne'er-do-well buddy, Freemont, dead and himself shot? At least Dad admitted he wasn't thinking straight. What excuse did that leave Tyler for participating in the cover-up and not telling her about it, but running away instead? He, too, claimed he did it for her. She could do without such pointless sacrifice and hollow mercy.

Her cell phone began to sound, but Jen ignored the insistent tone. Her dad? Tyler? Captain Mackey? No matter. She didn't care to talk to anyone right now. Besides, she was pulling into Mount Airy. The four-hour trip from Gatlinburg to her small hometown had passed in a blink of misery.

Jen guided her rental car down the familiar main street lined mostly by brick buildings—some of them sporting colorful murals—that held artsy shops, nostalgic restaurants and down-home staples like banks and hardware stores. Mount Airy advertised itself as the quintessential Mayberry and did a healthy tourist trade. Already this spring, the streets bustled with unfamiliar faces. Thankfully, her family home was well away from the seasonal crowds of vacationing strangers.

Soon she left the business district behind and turned the car onto a narrow, little-traveled road that led higher into the Great Smoky Mountains and within a mile ended in a private neighborhood barely clinging to the fringes of the town. Only four houses lined the cul-de-sac. Two had belonged to elderly people she'd known growing up but which were now occupied by young couples with small children, as evidenced by a few children's outdoor toys scattered on the healthy green lawns. At this time of day, the parents were likely at work and the children at day care or school.

Jen turned her attention to the other side of the street. One of the houses, a stucco dwelling—unusual for the area and in need of a coat of paint—used to belong to Tyler but had long been someone else's property. Then there was her family home that had belonged to generations of the Blackwell family but now stood vacant...and violated.

Jen suppressed a shudder at what she'd been

told about the carnage an intruder had left in-side. Rocks popped softly under the tires as she pulled the car into the short, gravel drive-way, never taking her eyes off the pale blue, clapboard structure. The curtained windows of her second-story bedroom peered down at her. What would she find inside?

Gulping down a lump in her throat, she put her hand on the door latch of her vehicle. Then, from the passenger seat, her cell phone chimed with the notification of a text message. With a huff, she scooped the phone up. She had a missed call from Captain Mackey, and failing to connect with her, he had sent a text.

The guard at your father's door says you left in the wee hours. I trust you're lying low some-where. Notify the department if there's any-thing we can do.

The captain had also sent a photo. It was a close-up of a sheet of paper. No doubt the one that had been in the mystery envelope deliv-ered to her work desk. The words spelled out in block letters sent a chill cascading down Jen's spine.

Do You Feel Safe?

She ground her molars together. The evil killer was sending the message that he could get to her even inside police headquarters.

Another text from Mackey popped up on her screen.

The test results on the powder came in. Common household flour.

A tight knot inside of Jen sprang loose, and she let out a huff. Then the only poison contained in the killer's taunting message was a toxin for the psyche. Whoever was behind all this was clever as well as vicious. Jen firmed her jaw. She would not be intimidated.

Jen texted the captain back, acknowledging receipt of the messages and thanking him, but not offering any clue to her whereabouts. Tucking her cell into the slot on her waist belt next to her pistol, she opened her car door and eased herself outside into the refreshing cool of a spring morning. With sharp eyes, she scanned the area for any evident threat. Birdsong greeted her, and a squirrel scampered up the trunk of the mature oak tree on her front lawn. All appeared as peaceful as a pastoral picture postcard, complete with majestic green mountain heights in the background.

Satisfied, Jen went up her front steps onto

the porch and inserted her key into the high-end lock she'd had installed on the front door when her dad went to the care home. She turned the key and stepped into the small foyer. Deliberately keeping her eyes averted from any damage that might be in sight, she turned toward the keypad beside the door that would neutralize the alarm.

Bile hit the back of her throat. As the caretaker David reported the intruder had destroyed the unit. The plastic casing had been smashed as if with a hammer or heavy object, and the wires had been ripped loose. Disconnected ends stuck out in every direction like a bad hair day. Whoever broke in also had the tech savvy to stop the system from notifying the monitoring service that the alarm box had been savaged. That fact fit with someone who could delete footage at her father's care home. Everything about this guy displayed a dichotomy of out-of-control rage and calculated intelligence. Tremors cascaded through Jen.

Get a grip, girl. Jen inhaled a long breath, let it out slowly then turned away from the useless alarm keypad. Stepping forward, she peered through the wide opening to her right that led into the living room.

A gasp stalled in her throat that had suddenly become as tight as if someone had a death grip on her neck. The caretaker had not exaggerated the devastation the intruder had wrought. The furnishings were all slashed and upended, and the curtains on the picture window were torn, the rod hanging askew. Every decoration had been stripped and flung carelessly. Even sections of wall sported holes as if smashed by a large fist. At least the family photos that had enjoyed pride of place on the mantelpiece were safe in her father's room at the care home. Here and there were signs that crime scene techs had done their best to dust for prints and search for evidence. What did the rest of the place look like if this area was so severely damaged? Jen's insides roiled.

Then gravel crunched under tires in her driveway, and the hairs at the base of her neck stood on end. She had company.

Scarcely daring to breathe, Jen crept through the debris to peer out the edge of the front window. A familiar pickup truck sat behind her vehicle, and a tall figure climbed out onto her lawn. A sensation like a warm shower flooded over her.

Tyler.

As much as she didn't *want* to see him, she also *needed* to see him. She'd never considered herself a contradictory creature, but at this moment, *conflicted* didn't begin to describe her emotions. What was wrong with her that she could be so angry with him and yet so hungry for his presence at the same time? She might as well wave the white flag right now. If she were honest with herself, she'd never gotten over him, which spelled impending shipwreck for her emotions. How could anything ever be right between them?

Tyler's head swiveled this way and that, scoping out the area. Then he moved toward the porch, his confident stride belying the pallor on his frowning face.

Suppressing a growl, Jen picked her way back to the foyer and flung open her front door. "You might as well come in and join the party. It's been a doozy."

She stood aside as Tyler entered the house. His wary gaze locked on hers. "Jen, I—"

"Stop!" She raised a hand, palm out. "I don't want to hear a word out of you. How did you find me?"

A grin played across his lips. "I thought you didn't want me to speak."

She narrowed her eyes at him. "The ice you're skating on is thinner than you can possibly imagine." His Adam's apple quivered. Good, he was nervous. "I meant I don't want to hear from you about past terrible decisions. Not yet. I'm still processing."

"Fair enough. I found you because I couldn't think of anywhere else you would go, especially knowing your home needed attention."

"Congratulations, you're a detective. Now let's go *detect* areas we can clean up."

She turned away and began to head back into the living room, but a touch on her arm stopped her. Scowling, she peered up at Tyler.

His wounded gaze nearly pierced the armor she'd erected around her heart. What did he have to be hurt about compared to finding out her beloved and trusted father was a secret criminal and her best friend and first love had betrayed her?

"If *I* can figure out where you went, don't you think this nameless, faceless enemy we're facing can do the same?"

"Bring it. I'm not hiding. If he shows up, we'll nab him."

She turned on her heel and led the way into the trashed living room where she stretched out her arms theatrically. "Behold—"

With a crash, the picture window shattered. Glass sprayed everywhere. Shards stung Jen's forehead, cheeks and arms. A fat canister sailed through the opening and landed at her feet.

"Grenade!" Tyler sprang into motion. He scooped Jen into his arms and dove behind the upended couch, wrapping himself around her like a human shield.

With a pop and a hiss, acrid black smoke began to fill the room. Eyes stinging, Tyler coughed. Not a fragmentation grenade, then. A frag would have detonated, spewing high-velocity shrapnel in every direction. Even the couch would have made a sorry shield. A smoke grenade was hard on the eyes and the lungs, but it wasn't designed to kill instantly. Nevertheless, they needed to find fresh air.

Hacking and wheezing, Jen wriggled free of his grip. "Kitchen." She crawled away from him.

Tyler followed on his hands and knees. Through watering eyes he squinted against the irritating smoke, and could barely make out her slender figure in the bitter cloud of blackness billowing through the room. Scrambling across the floor, they made it through the doorway into the marginally clearer kitchen area. As if of one mind, they scooted behind the kitchen island and found significantly fresher air. Had oxygen ever tasted so sweet?

"We could escape…out the back door." Jen gasped as she blinked rapidly, wiping dampness from her cheeks.

Some of that wetness was red from assorted cuts on her cheeks and forehead. Even her bare arms trickled thin worms of blood. Thankfully, nothing spurted. Tyler had been behind her in the doorway and had avoided taking any glass to his exposed body parts. His hands fisted against the impulse to address Jen's wounds. They had no time for triage or first aid.

"Don't you think...our assailant is expecting that?" His halting voice came out like he had gravel in his chest—exactly the way his lungs felt at this moment. "And he's shown... his willingness to shoot...with bow or gun."

"Higher ground, then." Her suggestion ended in a coughing session.

With a nod, Tyler pulled his pistol from its holster. Jen did the same and led out toward the staircase in a crouching scuttle. They had to pass through a thin wall of smoke that set them coughing again, but they reached the stairs and found them clear. The passage would bring them into the middle of the second floor with her parents' former bedroom on one side, Jen's childhood bedroom on the other and a bathroom straight ahead. At least they had the advantage of familiarity with their surroundings. Then again, their assailant had also been here when he trashed the place, so maybe not such an edge after all.

Moving sideways, Tyler kept a lookout behind them while they ascended as quickly as their heaving lungs allowed. At the base of the stairs, a dark-clad figure appeared out of the haze, wearing a gas mask and breathing as if through scuba gear. A sensation like salamander feet scampered up Tyler's spine. The man hefted a compact semiautomatic rifle in position to fire. He hadn't seen them yet, but Tyler and Jen were bottlenecked targets in the stairwell.

Tyler bumped Jen's back with his shoulder, urging her to greater speed. She responded without question, and they reached the top of the stairs even as the attacker below swiveled his rifle in their direction.

"Dive!" Tyler cried out.

As bullets chewed up the stair boards, they hurled themselves forward flat onto the floor then rolled in opposite directions out of the sightline of the stairs. If Tyler didn't know better, he'd think he was fighting alongside a trained ranger buddy. Jen was amazing. Then again, the two of them always had been so in tune that they nearly read each other's minds.

"You okay?" His focus remained on the stairwell, but his peripheral vision sought any sign that she'd caught a bullet.

"Fine. You?" Her voice sounded as if she was gargling sawdust.

"Dandy. I'll keep this guy at bay while you

call for help." Tyler took up a firing position flat on his stomach, gun aimed at the top of the stairs. If the shooter poked his head up, Tyler would blow it off.

Without a verbal response, Jen pulled out her phone. Perhaps she couldn't make another effort to speak. Her breathing rasped like a buzz saw.

"Hey, bozo!" Tyler called down to the shooter. "You'd better take off while you can. We've got help com—"

"No, we don't." Jen's urgent words halted Tyler's declaration. "No signal."

Every hair on Tyler's head stood to attention. A signal blocker? Who was this guy to have such resources? But then, anyone who had back channels to source C-4 could probably get their hands on fancy tech, too.

A throaty chuckle wafted up from below, eerily audible even through the hissing of the gas mask. "Trapped, are you?"

Another wave of hair-prickling electricity passed through Tyler. If this guy could sound any eviler, he didn't know how. Too bad for him and Jen, the lowlife's actions matched his threatening sounds. And, worse, Tyler couldn't recognize the voice filtered through the mask, so he still had no idea who they were up against. But the guy was wrong about one thing. He and Jen weren't trapped.

Tyler rapped lightly on the floorboards to get Jen's attention. From a few feet away from him on the opposite side of the landing her reddened eyes stared back at him from a face smeared with blood and grime. He couldn't afford for their adversary to hear what they were planning, so he flicked a pair of fingers toward Jen's bedroom behind her. She nodded understanding. He pointed at himself and then toward the stairwell. Comprehension filled her eyes. He would hold off the attacker while she escaped through a side window and down the sturdy trellis to the ground.

She shook her head vehemently. Then she reversed the hand signals with herself guarding the stairs against hostile approach while he escaped through the bathroom window onto the garage roof and from there to the ground. Both were clandestine exits Tyler had known her to use in their mischievous past. What teenager didn't know how to sneak out of their parents' house when they wanted to stay out later than they should?

Tyler huffed exasperation and motioned toward his broad shoulders. Maybe he could have fitted through the bathroom window as a lanky kid, but not as an adult. And her parents' bedroom behind him had no handy trellis outside the window offering him a safe way to the ground. Nor could he cross the stairwell opening to join her in escaping through *her* window. Not without passing in front of deadly fire from below. No, Jen needed to get away and summon back-up. Clearly, she understood his reasoning because she slumped and bit her lip, then jerked a nod, yielding to necessity.

As Jen crept away toward her bedroom, Tyler focused on the stairway. "How about you come on up here?" he asked their adversary. "We have a lot to discuss."

Feet shuffled near the bottom of the stairs. "How about you know when you're beaten and surrender? This can go the easy way or the hard way."

"Talking in clichés now? Maybe we should start with introductions. Obviously, you know who Jen and I are, but who are you? And don't say, 'your worst nightmare,' because you're not."

Well, maybe he was fudging the truth there. He'd been in plenty of tight situations in the Rangers, but nothing involving the woman he loved more than life itself. Now that he'd found her again, how could he ever let her go? Could she forgive him for choosing to walk away from her? Grievous problems for another day—if they had another day.

The questions and forebodings blew from

his head with the roar of their adversary's rifle spewing bullets up the stairway. Wood and plaster pelted Tyler, and he kept his head down. The moment the barrage ceased, Tyler rolled out into view of the stairwell and sent a trio of bullets toward the ground floor. A yelp said he'd either hit the guy or scared him. Hopefully the former, but probably the latter because he hadn't been able to spot the man as he fired. The vital thing was that he keep the shooter's attention off Jen's movements.

Where was she? Had she escaped the house on her way to summoning the police?

A high-pitched scream came from outside. *Jen!*

Panic drove Tyler to his feet, but wisdom kept him from darting without a plan in front of the open stairwell where a gunman lay in wait. *Now,* the risk of crossing the stairwell was warranted. Hauling in a deep breath, he held it as he sent another series of bullets toward his adversary even as he lunged for the opposite side of the hallway in the direction of Jen's room, where he could look out the window to see what was happening.

An ominous *tink-tink-tink* followed on his heels. He spared a look over his shoulder to spy a round object, hurled from below, rolling on the landing. *Not* a gas canister this time. A frag grenade. With a hoarse cry, Tyler dove through the doorway into the bedroom and hit the floor curled into a tight ball to protect his head and minimize his exposure.

An ear-numbing boom deafened him a split second later, and the wall ruptured between his vulnerable body and the hallway. Something large and hard—no doubt the mahogany chest of drawers that had been against the wall—slammed down onto his huddled body. Pain splintered through him, and blackness followed.

TWELVE

An acrid odor woke Jen from a place of absolute darkness. Gasoline fumes with a foul tang of smoldering plastic. Her eyes popped open, and the darkness within matched what she saw in the waking world. Nothing. The stench grew stronger in the warm stuffiness, and the warmth intensified by the second. Uncomfortably so. Her head throbbed, her body sweated and her eyes watered.

Where was she? What was happening?

Memories rushed in on her. She'd left the house via the trellis, which was nowhere near as sturdy as it had been when she was a teenager. Several boards broke under her feet as she moved, creating a hazardous descent, but she had finally reached firm ground. She'd rushed toward the front door. Taking out their assailant and ensuring Tyler's safety trumped any thought of running off to find help. Like retreat was ever her intention anyway.

She'd reached for the door handle, and something had struck her in the back with a sting like a massive mosquito, and an involuntary scream had left her lips. Ignoring the sensation, she'd plunged over the threshold, gun in hand. The smoke had largely cleared from the first floor, though residual tendrils drew a cough from her abused lungs. The dark-clad figure had stood at the foot of the stairs, still wearing a gas mask. As if in slow motion, the figure had hurled something up the stairs toward Tyler and then turned to her. She'd blinked, attempting to focus, but her whole mind had gone mushy. Lifting her gun to point it at the intruder was suddenly beyond her. She'd collapsed as an explosion above sent the world away.

Now, here she was. Wherever *here* might be.

A soft groan met her ears, and her breath caught. She wasn't alone.

"Tyler?" Jen croaked out through the arid desert of her throat.

She attempted to move but managed barely a twitch, as if her body were wrapped in cotton batting. Doubling down on her willpower, she managed to stretch out a hand, but not very far, because there was little room in this space that contained them. In fact, as sensation returned, it became clear they were stuffed into some sort of compartment. A vehicle trunk? Maybe, but the car was stationary. Her palm met cloth and a firm muscle beneath it. Sticky wetness also. Blood? Another groan, conveying pain, confirmed her suspicion.

The heat radiating into the compartment began to carry with it a suspicion of light, along with a soft crackling. Fire! This vehicle—if it was a vehicle—had caught fire.

Or had been set on fire.

They needed to get out immediately. But how? Shoving away the panic that attempted to grab her by the throat, Jen groped her surroundings. Her finger pads brushed metal, and she jerked her hand back with a gasp at the searing sensation. But she couldn't afford to halt her search. And then she had it, the trunk release.

The enclosing lid popped open with a deep *thunk*, and unnaturally heated air bathed her face. Night had fallen, and the flames surging from the vehicle did a spectral dance in the woodland surroundings. They appeared to be in a clearing surrounded by trees and had seconds to escape before the fire in the passenger compartment burst into the trunk and consumed them.

"Tyler!" She grabbed for his shoulders.

At her clawed fingers digging into his flesh,

he cried out and rolled over onto his back, eyes wide but vague and disoriented. She slapped his cheek as she scrambled out of the vehicle onto the ground. Her semi-numbed legs wouldn't hold her up, and she collapsed onto the blessedly cool earth.

No time to get comfortable. She shook herself and forced her legs to work. How she accomplished the feat, she had no idea. God's grace functioning through adrenaline?

Tyler was making valiant, grunting attempts to sit up. With the flames intent on embracing them both, she reached into the trunk, wrapped her arms around his torso just under his shoulders and heaved. They fell backward together, his heavy weight atop her. She ignored the crushing sensation, and with her arms and legs hugging him, she rolled them away from the burning car. As soon as the fresh air of the evening surrounded them, well away from the flames and gasoline fumes, she released Tyler—who rolled one more time like a tossed rag doll—and then she flopped spread-eagled in the lush and deliciously cool grass.

The hypnotic snap-crackle of fire and the ebb of adrenaline allowed lethargy to creep through her body. Her eyelids closed. A nap sounded like an excellent plan.

"Jen!" Someone snarled at her and prodded her shoulder.

Scowling, she forced her eyes open. "Wha'?"

Tyler's anxious face hovered over hers. Ruddy reflection from the dancing flames rendered his features macabrely fluid.

"Thank you for hauling us out of that funeral pyre, but we've got to get under cover." The thin hoarseness in his voice told the tale of their harrowing day. "Someone set that vehicle alight, and they could still be nearby to ensure we're goners."

The sense of his words got through to her, and Jen physically pinched herself, yelped and forced herself to sit up. Her muscles ached like she'd been thoroughly pummeled, but more likely her body's protests came from being bundled carelessly into a trunk and left there for hours in a cramped position. Hours? For sure. It hadn't even been lunchtime when they were attacked, and now it was after dark.

She patted herself down and discovered, as she'd expected, that whoever kidnapped them had left her with neither a cell phone or a weapon. No doubt Tyler was similarly without means to call for help or defend them.

Jen scanned the sky overhead. A starless, moonless night, which meant thick cloud cover. Was rain imminent?

"It's going to rain soon," Tyler answered her question without her having to voice it. "We need to find shelter. If that's possible. I don't know where we are."

"Me, either. Some type of wilderness seems a given."

"Which leaves a lot of wide-open spaces to consider. There are millions of acres of wilderness in the Great Smoky Mountains, much less the wider Appalachian chain. But maybe we're closer to civilization than we think. Or else how did the car get here?" Tyler heaved himself to his feet with a groan and stood swaying.

Jen sucked in a breath. How badly was he hurt? She got up and reached for him. Tyler hissed and backed away, clutching his left arm to his torso.

"A fragmentation grenade exploded on the landing of your house and slammed your heavy mahogany dresser down on top of me. The dresser took most of the shrapnel, but I think it broke my arm. Maybe even a rib or two." He turned and headed for the tree line with the exaggeratedly careful gait of the very drunk…or the extremely hurting.

"Your back is bleeding, also." Jen moved out in his wake, staying close in case it seemed like he was about to keel over. "Either the stitches ripped from your earlier back injury or some of the grenade shrapnel or debris must have hit you."

Tyler answered with a soft grunt. "If I'm not bleeding out, we're not going to worry about it right now."

As they moved into the trees, Jen smiled at the level of his wilderness savvy. An unerring woodsman, even in deep darkness, he'd directed their feet onto a sliver of a path most likely blazed by deer. Thus they avoided the extra effort of having to forge their own trail through thick brush and tangled tree limbs.

Even so, stray branches poked and prodded their progress. But what were a few scratches compared to being burned alive? Jen could only be thankful they'd escaped the flaming car, though she wouldn't mind a little extra light to aid their stumbling progress.

Suddenly, a large figure erupted from the thick brush near the path and stampeded away from them. A smaller figure rushed away on its heels. Jen squelched a shriek behind one hand clapped to her mouth and the other to her chest. They had inadvertently flushed a doe and her fawn from their hide.

"Let's take it," Tyler whispered.

"Take what?" Jen whispered back.

If only their soft conversation didn't sound so alien to the nocturnal sounds of nature. Any enemies out there could tell the difference and follow where they went.

"Oh-h-h," Jen barely breathed out as Tyler led the way into the branch-sheltered grotto so recently occupied by the deer. The animals' warmth and even their musky scent hung in the air.

Tyler gingerly let himself down to a sitting position with his side against a tree trunk. Almost as soon as Jen settled beside him, a spattering like the first sizzle of grease on a griddle commenced around them. Rain on the leaves.

Within minutes, the spatter became a muted roar, and with the intensifying rain came colder air. Jen moved closer to Tyler on his good side, and he wrapped his right arm around her shoulders. She didn't resist as he drew her head onto his shoulder. Very little of the water reached their protected spot. She sighed. How she had missed this man's arm around her.

"At least it's not a thunderstorm." She snuggled closer.

They jumped as a great boom and a flash of lightning punctuated her statement.

"Spoke too soon." Tyler's chuckle tickled her ear. "At least if an enemy lurks nearby, they won't be looking for us until the storm passes."

"*An* enemy?" The question popped from her

lips as her consciousness came to a sudden realization. Jen stiffened, and she lifted her head
from the sturdy shoulder. "I think we've made
a wrong assumption."

"What do you mean?"

"We both saw the assailant with the gas
mask who attacked us inside the house. We
weren't thinking about it then, but wasn't he
taller than five feet, eight inches?"

"You could be right about that."

"There's more. After I climbed down the
trellis, I raced through the front door to take
out gas-mask guy from behind. He was standing right in front of me at the foot of the stairs.
So who shot me in the back with a tranquil-
izer dart?"

Tyler sat frozen with his mouth open. A
stray drop of rain made it through their bushy
cover to plop onto his nose. He swiped the
moisture away with his fingers.

"Of course, there are two of them. They're
pooling their resources and working together
to bring us down. That's how the almost im-
possibly tight timeline works between the attack on Jarod at the care home and the murder
of his financial advisor, along with the staging
of his body. One was at the care home, while
the other attacked Mr. Gillespie."

Jen huffed. "Then who are they? From witness descriptions, we know it wasn't Randy Givens at my dad's assisted living home, but Randy could certainly be the brute who killed Arthur Gillespie and left his body for me to find on the trail. He could also be the guy in the gas mask with the automatic weapon."

"A definite possibility. Do you have any speculation as to who the accomplice could be?"

"I'm baffled. Though I suspect that if Randy is involved as the muscle, he's the sidekick, not the other way around. The mystery guy must be the brains of the operation. Randy couldn't reason his way out of a paper bag, though there's not much he wouldn't do for the right reward."

"Your deductions will get no argument from me. Let's try to rest. We'll likely think better in the morning."

Tyler shivered in the chilly air, and a speckle of fresh lacerations across his upper back throbbed in time with the earlier wound that had been sutured. He must have groaned, because Jen laid a gentle hand on his good arm.

"I wish we had a first aid kit so I could treat your injuries. And some light so I could even see them. Dawn can't come soon enough."

Tyler kept his reservations about that statement to himself. Dawn was likely to bring a whole new raft of dangers and complications. Was the deadly duo out there and in a position to continue their attacks come daylight? For that matter, where had they deposited him and Jen? Reaching civilization and getting help was imperative. Jen appeared to be in good shape physically, but would he have the stamina for a prolonged wilderness trek? Doubtful. But they would do whatever they needed to do. He wasn't about to surrender to a couple of lowlifes.

"Tip the moisture on some of these leaves into your mouth."

Jen's words broke Tyler out of his dark study. She was tapping into her survival skills. He needed to get his wits about him and do the same. The movement hurt, but the cool rain-water soothed his throat, and a measure of strength returned to his limbs.

He felt rather than saw Jen curl into a ball by his side and settle in. Tyler attempted to relax, but the pain was likely to keep him at least semi-awake. He fell into a cycle of brief alertness, prompted by the need to evaluate one forest sound or another for danger, and nebulous dreams featuring himself and Jen dodging between the trees avoiding a name-less threat. Too close to reality to write off as simple nightmares.

Finally, the sharp snap of a breaking twig jerked Tyler to full awareness. Something large approached. He held his breath, straining his senses for more indications of who or what it might be. A soft chuffing of breath carried to him like a creature sniffing deeply. His tense muscles relaxed. The doe most likely, checking to see if the intruders had left. They hadn't. The muted thud of hooves and the swish of disturbed undergrowth signaled the creature's retreat.

Dawn was breaking, evidenced by his ability to make out his surroundings in a growing illumination. Jen lay curled at his side in a nest of undergrowth. She shivered slightly in her sleep, a testament to the cool morning temperatures. Her blond bun had become a charming rat's nest. Loose tendrils of hair feathering around her face. Dark lashes nestled against pale cheeks, and her breath disturbed tendrils of grass in a steady rhythm.

How he loved this woman. He'd wanted to spend his life at her side. But he'd loved her enough to walk away for her sake. Would she ever see his decision that way?

As if his steady gaze reached through her sleep, Jen opened her eyes and looked up at him. Softness and welcome gazed back at him, and his heart swelled. Then she blinked, and her whole expression turned remote and clinical. She sat up.

"How are you this morning?"

Tyler swallowed a bitter chuckle. At least she cared enough to ask.

"I haven't tried to move yet, so the pain is steady but bearable. We don't have the luxury of remaining still, however, so I'll have to manage regardless."

"Is there anything I can do?"

"Help me rig my belt into a sling for my broken arm. Then I won't have to hold on to it with my other one and can have a hand free."

Involuntary groans accompanied the activity, but at last Tyler's arm was somewhat immobilized.

"We need to get going." He leaned forward, working up the will to brave the pain and move.

"What about the wounds on your back?"

"There's still nothing we can do for them. Not even clean them unless we come across a stream somewhere. Best let them be. I don't think they're bleeding anymore."

Jen's expression darkened. "You'll let me know if that changes."

"Aye-aye, Cap'n."

"Don't get fresh with me, Tyger."

The hint of a smile on her lips lifted Tyler's spirits. He closed his lips tight against any wounded outcry as he crawled out of their borrowed deer sanctuary and rose to his feet on the narrow game trail.

Jen followed him out and stood looking around. "At least the storm passed on in the night, and we won't have to contend with rain while finding our way out of the forest. Shall we continue down the path?"

Tyler shook his head. "I want to return to the clearing. There must be enough of a road to allow the car access. When we see the direction the road goes, we'll know which direction we should go."

"Even though we won't necessarily want to be right *on* the road if our adversaries have laid a trap."

"We'll have to balance the need for ease of passage with the need for caution, but yes, that's the idea."

"Right. Follow me." She led the way in stealth mode toward the clearing.

Though the awkwardness of Tyler's injuries gave him the sensation that he was lumbering like an ox, neither of their footfalls made more than a whisper of sound. Soon, they stood at the edge of the woods, peering at the burned-out shell of a sedan with its trunk lid gaping open. The rain had thoroughly extinguished the fire and largely cleansed the air, but a taint lingered in the area. Only time would completely eradicate the scent of scorched metal and burned rubber.

Tyler's gaze left the derelict vehicle and dissected the clearing and the woods surrounding it. As he'd suspected, a rough and overgrown road—hardly more than a pair of wheel depressions among weeds—led away in a direction perpendicular to where he and Jen stood. However, neither sight nor sound of other human presence remained. Maybe the attackers were convinced their victims were dead and had left the area.

Then a fluttering object across the clearing grabbed his attention, and his heart seized. Next to him, Jen gasped and grabbed his arm. She'd seen the same thing. An arrow held a sheet of paper to a tree trunk.

"Maybe the paper was there all along," Jen murmured.

Tyler shook his head.

"Of course not," she continued. "The storm would have torn it to shreds."

On cautious feet, they skirted the clearing until they reached the arrow and its attached note. Swallowing against a dry throat, Tyler snatched the sheet free and pulled it close enough for them both to read.

"Chattier than the other communications." Jen's tone held more anger than fear.

We're delighted you escaped our little roaster.
    We'd hoped you would,
which was why we didn't tie you up.
    More fun this way.
LET THE HUNT BEGIN!

Heart pounding, Tyler pulled Jen into the cover of the trees. They hunkered down near a pine tree behind the cover of a set of tangled bushes. He stretched his senses to detect a hostile presence but got nothing. That situation would surely soon change. For them, safety was an illusion. His jaw firmed. Their hunters needed to find out the tables could easily turn. How he and Jen could make that happen, Tyler had no idea, but they needed to think of something fast.

THIRTEEN

Swallowing deeply, Jen hugged herself. Shivers rattled her that had nothing to do with the morning chill. The words of the jovially venomous note replayed in her head. Who *were* these sick creeps?

If only she had some way beyond conjecture to determine if Randy Givens was involved. Then they could be assured they were dealing with at least one familiar and to some extent predictable element. Then again, whoever was the team's brains had directed events in startling ways that kept her and Tyler on the defensive. On the other hand, by years of childhood experience with the guy, she and Tyler had some idea of how to press Randy's buttons to glean a certain response that might override the smarter one's directives. Then it came to her.

"Tyler."

His head swiveled toward her.

"Remember how much Randy loved bow-hunting?"

"Another indication he's involved."

"No, a certainty. Let's backtrack a bunch of years. Randy used to consider himself our rival during bowhunting season, and he liked to flaunt his equipment. Now, fast-forward to us dodging arrows at the national park. Remember I saw a flash of blue through the trees. Randy's favorite bow—a crossbow—has a neon blue stripe. It was him."

"Good enough for me." Tyler jerked a nod. "Should we expect he'll be hunting us with it?"

"I think it's a strong possibility. He seemed happy to throw grenades and shoot at us in the house, but out in the woods, he may feel it a matter of pride to use the bow."

"You're reading him well, I'm sure, but we won't count on it. Especially with this unknown guy in the mix. He may prefer to put bullets into us. What are our resources to survive?"

Jen's stomach curdled. "Precious few."

Tyler took her hand and cupped it in his calloused palm. "Precious indeed."

The wealth of warmth in his gaze robbed Jen of breath. Was he saying that their love for each other was a weapon against their enemies? To her way of thinking, the emotional attachment could too easily be a liability. *Whoa!* What was she thinking? Jen mentally shook herself. The time for the L-word between them was long gone. Wasn't it?

She withdrew her hand. "They may have taken our phones and guns—"

"And my knife."

His rueful, lopsided grin plucked at her heart, and she turned away to scan their surroundings.

"And your knife," she acknowledged. "But we still have our wits and wilderness savvy."

"What are those telling you?"

"Under our circumstances, wilderness wisdom would call for two things. One, we need water, or we will soon grow weak. The deer trail is the most likely to lead us to water. Two, we need to get *out* of the wilderness. We don't have the equipment to stay, and you need medical care. The vehicle track is the best route to find civilization—or at least a well-traveled road where someone might stop for us."

"I agree, and that's a conflict. Common sense, otherwise known as wits, would tell us our adversaries will be waiting somewhere along the vehicle track to pick us off as we seek help."

Jen nodded. "If we don't show up because we've gone to find water, they might get rattled and come back this way looking for us.

Randy will, for sure. He's got no patience. Then maybe we can sneak around them."

"The game trail it is, then."

He started to rise, but Jen caught him by the wrist.

"Are you sure you're up to it?"

"I'll have to be up to a little trekking, and probably a whole lot more activity than that before we get out of here." His lips compressed in a thin line. Whiteness on the edges of his mouth conveyed the pain he was in, but his gaze held solid determination.

A truth struck her, and her heart skipped a beat. She knew the measure of this man, his courage, his integrity. In her mind, she'd characterized him as cowardly for running away from her. How could that be right?

"Did you really leave Mount Airy all those years ago for my sake?" The question popped out of her mouth without conscious volition.

Raw emotion flared on Tyler's face. If she'd seen physical pain there a moment ago, now she read an inner agony of soul that dwarfed any bodily discomfort.

"What else could I have done?" His voice had gone hoarse. "The law-and-order part of me said I should turn your dad in, but that would have ruined both your lives. And for what? A conviction and prison time for ultimately stealing nothing and paying with a bullet wound and losing his partners in crime? One of them his own brother-in-law? Besides, Jarod had been like a father to me, and you… you were anything *but* a sister to me. I could stick around and play along with the cover-up—attempt to deceive you every day for the rest of our lives. But I couldn't live that way, and I knew you'd figure out secrets were being kept. Then you'd hate me—hate both of us."

As if a giant fist held her in its grip, Jen could hardly breathe. "So you left." Her voice emerged as a wisp of sound.

Tyler hung his head. "I was in turmoil. No matter what I chose to do, you got hurt."

"You got hurt, too. No matter what you did."

Even as she said the words, the simple truth burst upon Jen like a shower of sparks. Through no fault of his own, Tyler had been placed in an impossible position. Whether she agreed with his ultimate solution or not, he'd acted in what he believed to be her best interest at great cost to himself.

A hard place within Jen's core softened slightly. She was still angry. Furious, even. But she'd been focused exclusively—selfishly— on her own wounding and hadn't recognized the suffering of others. Given time, maybe some measure of resolution could eventually be found after all. If they lived long enough.

"The deer trail, then." She rose to her feet and headed in that direction, skirting the edge of the woods to maintain a degree of cover.

Jen sensed more than heard Tyler following. No archer or gunman took a shot at them, but the moment-to-moment threat pulsed around them like a living thing. She didn't take a full breath until they entered the game trail and continued deeper into the forest. They moved, single file, without another word and almost without a sound of any kind. If not for the occasional pained hiss when they crossed a rough patch, Jen might have wondered if she'd lost him.

The pungent odor of moist earth and leaf mulch teased her nostrils. Blooming spring wildflowers splashed color onto the forest green and wood brown. Foliage swished in the breeze, and branches creaked. Here, a rodent squeaked. There, a squirrel's claws went *snickety-snick* up a tree trunk. Nothing indicated a hostile human presence. Because of the dense forestation, their adversaries must get close to take shots at them. No opportunity for sniping, as there might be if they were on the vehicle track.

Within ten minutes, a new sound entered the

chorus of natural forest noises. The swoosh of running water. Instantly, the dryness of Jen's throat turned acute. If only she had a taste of the life-giving liquid this instant. Her feet wanted to hurry, but Jen made them slow down instead. The volume of the moving water grew steadily. They weren't approaching a mild stream but a rushing river, heavy with spring runoff. Perhaps a danger in itself.

Gaze firmly forward, Jen lifted a foot to take a step, but a fist closed around her arm and pulled her back. She gasped and turned to find Tyler hanging on to her. He nodded toward the ground in front of them. She followed his gaze and sucked in a breath. The jaws of a set bear-trap gaped with serrated jaws to clamp on the leg of any creature foolish enough to step into it.

"Thank you." She laid a hand over his on her arm. "I should have been watching where I planted my feet."

Brows drawn together in thunder mode, Tyler released her and picked up a thick branch from the forest floor. Stepping around her, he poked the branch into the maw of the trap. The jaws closed with a violent snap, and the branch shattered.

Jen jumped and shivered. "A little gift from our adversaries, no doubt."

"A danger to human *and* beast." Tyler flung the remainder of the branch into the underbrush.

Hot anger spurted through Jen as she shuddered at an image of the fawn's delicate leg stepping into the sharp jaws. The human scent around the trap perhaps steered them away from the certain death sentence.

"Water up ahead." Tyler tilted his head toward the sound. "That's probably why these jokers thought this was a good place to sabotage."

He moved out in the lead. They both proceeded more cautiously now. At last they came to the edge of the forest, but not on the riverbank. Instead, they stood atop a cliff, looking down on the river about twenty feet below. The game trail led down the cliffside along a steep route only sure-footed, four-legged creatures could follow. Or two-legged creatures with a pair of good arms to assist them.

Jen turned her gaze toward Tyler, who had come up beside her. Under the morning sun, his face had an unhealthy gray caste. Sweat glistened on his skin, though the air was cool enough to make her wish for a jacket. They'd never even looked at the shrapnel wounds on his back, which could be starting to fester. But like he'd said, without medical supplies or liquid to cleanse the wounds, there had been no point in attempting first aid in the night. Now, in daylight, she could at least look, possibly even pick out the most surface of any foreign objects, and then wash the lacerations. If they could get to the water.

Or if she could bring some to him.

Her heart did a little flip as her gaze lit upon a man-made object half-buried in the soil at the base of the cliff. The item told her two things. One, a careless camper had lost their canteen, or it had washed down the river to this point from somewhere upstream. And two, therefore, this forest area couldn't be far from places frequented by people. Lots of Appalachian wilderness knew no human presence. Even the overgrown track where their captors had driven the car might have existed only as a long-forgotten logging road far from so much as a trekker's campsite.

"Look!" She pointed at the dented metal object below. "That hasn't been there long enough to get rusty. It should still hold water." *I hope.* "I'm going to go down, fill it and bring it back."

Tyler's gaze never turned from a focus on the steep wooded hill on the far side of the river from where they stood.

"Did you hear me?" Jen huffed and stepped out toward the descent. "I'm going—"

"It's a lure." Tyler's hand grabbed Jen's shirt and snatched her to him, even as a projectile hissed past the spot where she had been standing.

Jen's heart somersaulted into her throat as her gaze lit on movement at the edge of the trees beyond the river. A man rose from the brush, and if she could have made out the details of his face at this distance, no doubt she would have seen a big smile as he fitted another arrow into his bow.

"Run!" Tyler's shout rang in Jen's ears as he shoved her toward the forest.

Tyler lunged into the trees on Jen's heels, and the forest swallowed them. A spot between his shoulder blades tingled in expectation of piercing pain from an arrow. But no projectile lodged in him, although the shrapnel wounds on his back burned and stung. Warm trickles indicated that the punctures and lacerations had opened again. His arm ached like a rotten tooth. If they didn't get out of the forest soon and find help, their enemies would ensure his injuries ceased to matter.

Ahead of him, Jen slowed and stopped as they confronted a dense patch of forestation. They would either need to fight their way through thickly twined branches or change direction.

She stopped, turned toward him, and laid a hand on his shoulder.

"We can't run around aimlessly. Randy's partner is out here somewhere, and I doubt he's wielding a bow and arrow."

"Given the environment, I would guess a rifle would be his weapon of choice. I don't think he's near here, though."

"Why not?"

"Randy lurked to ambush us at the river if we chose that direction. It only makes sense that his cohort would be guarding the vehicle track."

Jen let out a soft groan. "Either way we travel, an armed killer awaits."

"That's *their* plan. We need one of our own. Any suggestions?"

"Randy will try to make his way to this side of the river. There must be a bridge somewhere. But it will take time for him to get close to us again. His partner is going to be watching the overgrown road. We need to move quickly and quietly through the woods and ambush the guy from a direction he doesn't suspect. If we can take possession of his gun, we stand a good possibility of getting away."

Tyler resisted the frown threatening to form on his face. "Good possibility" was not how he would describe their prospects, but he wouldn't discourage her optimism.

"First, we must move in close enough to identify his location. Then one of us will have to draw his attention while the other attacks and overpowers him."

"You're in no condition to do any attacking." Jen smirked. "Guess which role you get?"

Tyler opened his mouth to protest then shut it again. He started another protest then stopped, closed his mouth and hung his head.

Jen let out a small giggle. "You're gawping like a fish out of water." Her hand gripped his good arm, and she drew him close. "It'll be okay. I can do this."

Her gentle assurance warmed him deep on the inside. "I know you can. It's just my manly instinct not to *want* you to face that risk. I'll get over it."

"Don't worry. You'll have plenty of risk drawing the guy's fire until I can clobber him."

"Like the moves you pulled on that perp in the hospital parking lot?"

"Exactly."

She turned and melted away into the trees. Tyler followed, keeping her barely in sight as his senses quested for any sign of threat. She moved like a wisp of smoke. Tyler normally did, too, but his injuries dulled his woodcraft. His progress wasn't quite as lumbering as a buffalo, but try as he might, he couldn't match her stealth. Jen was right to assign him the role of distraction.

For long minutes, they traveled obliquely from the game trail in the direction of the road. The last traces of early morning fog dissipated, though the air remained damp and slightly chilly. Neither he nor Jen was dressed for wilderness trekking, but at least their constant movement staved off the shivers that would wrack the broken bone in his arm. The rich odor of years of leaf mulch on the forest floor teased his nostrils.

Up ahead, Jen raised her right arm, fist closed, in a sign to halt. Tyler went still and listened. A small rodent skittered beneath the mulch. Somewhere out of sight a woodpecker hammered a tree, and a meadowlark sang. But some other sound lurked on the very edge of audible.

Mumbling.

Yes, a human being was grumbling under their breath no more than twenty feet from where they stood. Jen turned and grinned at him. He grinned back. For all his concern about his own woodcraft, this guy had none.

Jen patted the air in a signal for Tyler to stay put and then she faded into the trees. Tyler held still, flesh prickling. The mumbling went on sporadically, and the normal forest noises continued, but he caught neither sight nor sound of Jen. A good indication that she was closing in on their target undetected.

A short eternity later, Jen materialized at his side. He looked a question at her.

"No rifle," she mouthed. "Handgun only."

Tyler's eyebrows climbed, but then he realized that if this guy was a native city-dweller, he might lack experience with a rifle. Of course, a handgun was just as deadly at close quarters, so he had to draw the guy's attention—possibly his fire—so Jen could perform a sneak attack. In that sense, he was doing his part to keep Jen safe in a relative sense. Nothing about this situation was remotely safe.

Tyler pointed in a direction that would take him beyond their adversary to a location where he would create a disturbance. Her expression somber, Jen nodded. She knew—they both knew—the next few minutes could spell the difference between life and death for them. He moved out, adrenaline lending him the capacity to recapture some of his grace in the environment.

Their enemy's mumbling had ceased, but now steady footfalls betrayed the guy was pacing. Impatient. Uncomfortable. Good for them, bad for him.

In a position to the man's right rear, Tyler

stopped and scanned his environment. A fist-sized rock lay near his feet. Carefully, he bent down—his wounds scolding him—and hefted the chunk of sandstone. Then he flung it into a clump of nearby bushes and squatted down to minimize any target he might make if the nervous guy started shooting indiscriminately.

The pacing sounds ceased, and the forest went still as if holding its breath. Tyler located another rock with his fingers and tossed it into the same clump of bushes.

"Randy, is that you?" Their adversary's voice emerged in a quivery whisper.

Tyler grinned. Not merely uncomfortable in the wilderness, this guy was downright scared. Maybe there was real hope for him and Jen yet.

"Randy, stop fooling around." The voice came out stronger, more natural. "There are bears and mountain lions out here."

Tyler didn't recognize the voice. Why would a stranger be involved in this mess with Randy Givens? A mystery to solve later.

He threw another rock, and a gunshot answered. Then sounds of a tussle. Another gunshot was followed by a pained cry.

Tyler hustled toward the fray. He emerged from the woods at the edge of the overgrown track, which turned out to be a V in the road with another overgrown track proceeding at a thirty-degree angle from the other. A few yards away, Jen wrestled on the ground with a man that matched the description of the fake nursing assistant from Jarod's care home, minus the beard. Jen's fists wrapped around the stranger's gun hand, keeping the weapon pointed away from their bodies, while she kicked and kneed the man. Grunts and yelps came from the wrestling pair. By their timbre, the cries of pain originated with Jen's opponent. A few strides brought Tyler to the edge of the skirmish, poised to kick the gun out of their enemy's hand.

"Stop!" A voice bellowed from the tree line. "Release him, Jennifer Blackwell, or I'll shoot Tyler where he stands."

The pair on the ground froze their activity. Tyler looked up to find Randy Givens, arrow nocked and bow drawn, staring them down from a position in the center of the road. The guy had a clear line of sight, and he was well within range. Their enemy wouldn't miss this time.

Givens had caught up with them much faster than anticipated. And now Tyler and Jen were going to die.

FOURTEEN

Jen stood beside Tyler on the track with her hands raised. Tyler only had one hand raised for obvious reasons. They were well and truly caught, and she didn't see a way out for them this time. Their enemies glared at them, one holding a bow and the other a pistol; one familiar face and one stranger.

Who *was* that other guy, and why was he involved? Would they even get the chance to know before they died?

She glanced up at Tyler. He smiled down at her. The warmth in his eyes spoke peace to her heart. At least she wasn't going to die alone. No, that trite thought didn't express her heart's meaning at all. Despite everything, she could be thankful she was leaving this earth in the company of the man she loved. The one she'd always loved. No matter what. She owed it to him to tell him so.

"Tyler, I—"

"No blood!" The unknown adversary screeched, pressing Randy's bow to the side.

His own pistol remained pointed at the ground. If she stood only a few feet closer to these creeps, Jen would have lunged at them for their inattention. Probably got shot with an arrow or a bullet for her trouble, but any opportunity was better than none.

"What are you talking about?" Randy sidled away from his partner and lifted his bow again.

"I told you why." The stranger's low snarl accompanied darted glances toward them and then back to Randy like he was trying to convey a message he didn't want her or Tyler to know.

"You're serious?" Randy turned a glare at his partner. "A guy who can make a bomb passes out at the sight of blood?"

The unidentified creep's free hand formed a fist, and his cheeks reddened. "I craft the explosive devices. I don't stick around to view the results. Thanks for ratting out my private foibles to our prisoners."

Next to her, Tyler's feet shifted. He shuffled forward almost without appearing to move.

"Are you for real, Winthrop?" Randy's tone carried a snarl. "I left you standing guard here to stop them if they came this way, but you had no intention of shooting them. What were you going to do? Talk them to death?"

Winthrop? First name or last name? Jen turned the name over and over in her mind like a blind person attempting to read braille faintly etched into a smooth rock. Did that name sound familiar? If so, the context eluded her.

The guy called Winthrop scowled. "I figured I'd point the gun at them, and they'd do anything I said."

Tyler inched forward, but Randy suddenly brought his bow up.

"None of that now." He glowered at Tyler. "I *will* shoot if you make me, and Win can pick his own sissy self up off the ground."

Jen felt more than saw her childhood friend's muscles stand down. He'd tried to act on her earlier impulse but realized the futility. Still, if the bickering between the bad guys had gone on a few seconds longer, he would surely have made the try—if only to give her the opportunity to get away. She knew Tyler like a well-worn book that never grew old.

"Don't call me names." Winthrop sulked. "I can't help it."

Randy snorted. "If you won't let me turn them into pincushions, what will we do with them? It's past the time for this to be over so we can get what we've got coming to us."

"What do you think you have coming to you, Randall Givens?" Jen challenged. "We don't owe you anything."

"Hah! You owe me big-time for bullying me on the playground. And that's just for starters."

Tyler's eyebrows climbed up his forehead. "*Us* bullying *you*? What reality were you living in?"

"Shut up, all of you." Winthrop lifted his pistol and pointed it at Tyler and Jen. "Like my colleague here, I *will* shoot if I must and sort myself out after." He glanced at his partner. "Trust me a little bit longer. I have the perfect solution."

Jen's skin crawled at the smarmy tone and the evil certainty in the man's eyes.

Randy huffed. "Like all these plans you've made have turned out great, huh? Now here we are, and they're still alive."

"Not for long."

"Where are we taking them?"

"You know."

Wordless communication passed between the plotters.

A grin bloomed across Randy's face. "Oh, yeah. I get you. That *is* perfect. Poetic-like."

Winthrop gestured with his pistol toward

the track veering away from the one that led to the clearing with the burned-out car that had nearly been her and Tyler's tomb. For long seconds, Jen's feet remained fixed on the ground. Whatever lay along the alternate track didn't sound like a destination they would welcome.

"Move!" Randy's bellow and a threatening gesture with his bow unstuck Jen's feet, and she took a small step in the required direction.

Tyler's hand found her elbow, and he gave a squeeze that communicated confidence though not necessarily the source for it.

"No touching," Winthrop snapped.

"No problem." Tyler waved a dismissive hand at their captors. "But it's not practical for us to walk along with our hands in the air. We'll need our arms for balance on this rough terrain."

"Fair enough." Randy jerked his chin in the affirmative. "Blackwell, you walk in front of me in one tire rut, and Cade, you walk in front of Win in the other rut. Now, stop stalling and march. We have a few miles to cover."

Jen's heart fell. As tired, thirsty, hungry, cold and achy as she was, Tyler's condition must be infinitely worse. She shot him a searching look, but he returned a nod from an impassive face.

Jen struck out up the abandoned, potholed

road. Her feet swished through weeds and crunched on the occasional bit of ground rock. This road must have been used more than the other branch to rate laying gravel. It probably led to somewhere more significant, or at least more useful, once upon a time.

Time went on, the sun rose higher and the day grew hotter. Sweat broke out on Jen's brow. She glanced in Tyler's direction to find him gritting his teeth as he huffed along. Very occasionally, a soft moan escaped his lips. If only she could spare him this agony. Why was he caught up in this business that seemed to center on the Blackwell family? If either of their competing theories held water, these people thought they could somehow get their hands on the Blackwell emerald mine, and/or Randy sought revenge for her dad's part in the botched casino robbery.

"The least you could do," she puffed out between labored breaths, "is to offer condemned prisoners the reason why they are about to die. And I know it has nothing to do with playground squabbles."

"Don't act so innocent, girly." Randy's tone dripped spite. "Your daddy set mine up, betrayed him and got him killed, and you helped him cover it up all these years."

Jen halted and whirled. "My father set no

one up. He betrayed no one. Never could he do such a thing."

Randy sneered with yellowed teeth. "Sure, sure. Far be it from a guy who could plan a heist to turn on his partners. Being so upright and law-abiding and all."

The sarcasm from her childhood nemesis shot heat through Jen's veins. Tyler's hand on her shoulder barely stopped her from launching herself at Randy.

"Your lowlife father lured my dad into the robbery plot," she ground out. "You know that's true. Dad never meant for anyone to get hurt."

Randy's face turned red as a hot stovepipe. "If I didn't think Win's solution would make you suffer more, I'd put an arrow in you right now. I lost myself when my dad got killed. Tried the Navy, washed out, then did a bunch of stupid things and went to prison." He spat out the words so fiercely that spittle flew from his mouth.

Illumination struck Jen. In the typical narcissist's convoluted logic, Randy's criminal behavior and subsequent incarceration were *her* dad's fault. Nothing to do with his own father's example or his own choices.

"Take responsibility for yourself." Tyler's quietly spoken words encapsulated Jen's new understanding with simple eloquence.

"What he said." She poked a thumb in Tyler's direction and continued along the track.

"For your information—" Tyler glanced over his shoulder "—until yesterday, Jen had no idea of her father's involvement in the attempted casino robbery. I'm the one who helped cover it up. It's why I left Mount Airy fourteen years ago."

Winthrop let out a snicker. "Thank you very much for the clarification, but that little detail makes no difference. You all have to go to pave our way to possess a mine like one of these."

The man waved before them as they entered a clearing containing an enormous rocky upheaval of ground. The rough contours of the cliff loomed at twice Tyler's height. A large hole in the rock face opened a dark mouth toward them.

Jen knew what she was looking at immediately. "An old emerald mine."

"Indeed, it is." Winthrop chuckled. "Petered out and abandoned long ago. Not like yours, my dear. They say the Blackwell mine is the richest strike ever in the northern hemisphere, rivaling even the mines in Colombia."

Jen rounded on him. "What is that to you when you have no claim?"

Winthrop wagged a finger at her. "Tut-tut. That would be telling. I'm not like some movie villain who needs to brag and explain himself before doing away with the pesky goody-goodies."

Tyler's lips spread in a grin. "At least you admit you're a villain."

The cocky little man gave a bow. "All my life. It's been a wild ride. Lots of ups and downs, but this will be my crowning achievement. Now get in there." All joviality gone from his expression, he pointed toward the cave's dark maw.

Something like a dark veil closed over Jen's vision, as if the very sunlight had dimmed several shades. With the dimming came a chill—inner, not outer. If they went into the cave, they would never come out.

Then a strong arm draped her shoulder and pulled her close. The familiar smell of suede leather with buttery sandalwood encompassed her, along with a faint tang of explosives and forest detritus from the events of the past twenty-four hours. Every scent and sensation was welcome and a counterpunch to the overwhelming dread.

"It'll be okay, darling." Tyler's soft voice and warm breath in her ear sent the dread scurrying.

"Sure, sure. It'll be okay." Randy let out a creepy laugh, and Winthrop's guffaw joined in the mockery.

Tyler's arm still around her shoulder, Jen allowed herself to be herded through the cave mouth. Randy slung his bow behind his back and took the pistol from his partner, who picked up an object from a nearby rock and clicked a switch. The LED lantern illuminated a significant circumference within what looked to be a rapidly narrowing passage. Winthrop also snatched up another item—a long, thick rope. Jen's already dry mouth turned Saharan as her imagination predicted dire things.

"After you." The man gestured deeper into the cave with the lantern.

Following a few minutes of twisting and turning and stumbling over the uneven floor, they arrived in a small, irregularly shaped cave room. The space was unspectacular, but one feature dominated the room—a square, man-made pit in the floor.

Winthrop gestured toward it. "Used to be an elevator shaft leading to the passages where the main deposit was found. When they shut down the mine, the underground passages were sealed off, and all the equipment was taken away, but the pit is all we need for our purposes today."

As he talked, he fastened the rope securely to an outcropping of rock sticking up from the floor. Then he tossed the rope's end down the shaft where it landed with a slight splash. He grinned—a smug look Jen was coming to hate.

"Yes, there are a few inches of water down below accumulated from seepage through the old passages. But I wouldn't drink it. Chemicals in there from the mining process and who knows what else. Probably kill you faster than thirst. But what do I know? Why don't you go down and check it out?"

Jen's breathing began to come in little gasps. "No."

The word burst from her as she flung herself toward the man with the lantern.

Winthrop's smirk morphed into an alarmed O. But a split second before the collision happened, Randy's lanky body crashed into hers. With a shriek, she went airborne, hurtling toward the dark pit.

Roaring a warning, Tyler threw himself between Jen's flying body and the pit's edge. She bounced off him and crumpled to the cave floor, but the impact staggered him backward. For pregnant moments, he scrabbled with his feet on the lip of the drop-off. Then he lost the battle and toppled over the edge.

The fall ended quickly in a splash of icy water geysering over his body as he hit the bottom sideways. Spluttering, Tyler lifted his head above the metallic-smelling liquid and found himself sitting in what amounted to only a couple feet of water. Thankfully he'd landed on his uninjured side, sparing his broken arm, and the water cushioned his fall into nothing worse than a mildly bruising impact with the solid stone bottom of the pit.

Above, Jen let out a panicked cry. "No, no, no, no, no!"

Her head poked over the edge, and then her whole body as she scrambled down the rope their captors had provided.

"Stay there, Jen," Tyler called, but he was too late.

She arrived at the bottom of the pit with him. Likely there was nothing he could have done to stave off her descent. Their adversaries would have tossed her in if she hadn't climbed down.

Jen squatted in front of him, heedless of the water. "Are you all right? Please say you're okay."

"I'm okay."

"You're not just saying that to ease my mind, are you?"

Despite the situation, Tyler chuckled. "Yes, I'm saying it, but I also mean it. Help me up."

She rose and lent him her hand so he could pull himself into a standing position. Even as they turned toward the rope, it rose rapidly out of the shaft. A pair of gloating faces peered down at them from above.

"Enjoy your spelunking adventure." Winthrop cackled.

"What he said," Randy seconded.

Then their heads withdrew, footsteps retreated and the light faded to nothing, leaving oppressive darkness and silence behind. Bone-rattling shivers wracked Tyler, sending shafts of pain throughout his body. He felt rather than saw Jen standing next to him, doing nothing but breathing. He pictured her with her fists balled and her teeth clenched.

Finally she let out a long sigh bearing the slightest hint of a whimper. "I didn't think our situation could get any worse, but now here we are."

"These guys have the biblical Joseph's brothers beat for villainy. I don't think they intend to come back and pull us out of the pit—even to sell us into Egyptian slavery."

Jen snorted. "You always did have the quirkiest sense of humor under pressure."

Her voice echoed slightly in the cavern above. Tyler reached out and drew her close. She nestled against his chest. If this were the end for them, at least they were together—the way they were always meant to be.

Jen mumbled something into the fabric of his sodden shirt.

"What was that?"

She lifted her head. "The sides of the shaft aren't smooth. I noticed that on my way down."

"You're not thinking about attempting to climb out, are you?"

"Not thinking. Doing."

She moved away from him. Shuffling and sloshing noises began, punctuated by occasional soft humming sounds.

"Okay, here's a spot. Stand against the wall as far from me as possible in case I lose my grip and fall back into the shaft. I don't want to slam into you."

Tyler complied, planting his back against a rock wall. "Slow and easy does it."

"More like swift and agile. The hand-and footholds are meager. I'll need to find fresh ones by feeling as quickly as possible and keep moving."

The next eternity passed in a cycle of climbing and falling and frustration. At last Tyler gathered her sodden, shivering, exhausted body close and ordered her to stand down. Jen went still, and her ragged breathing eventually quieted.

"You're hot. We're standing knee-deep in frigid water, and I can feel the heat radiating off you." She pressed a hand to his clammy forehead. "You're running a fever."

"Tell me something I don't know." He attempted a chuckle that ended with a groan.

She cupped his face in both hands. "I'm getting you out of here."

What Tyler wouldn't give to see that utterly Jen-like earnest determination in her eyes one more time, but at least he could imagine it. She pushed away from him and went back to hunting for that sweet spot that would provide enough hand-and footholds to bring her up and out of the pit.

This time the grunting and scrabbling went on and on, stretching seconds into minutes. Then came a muted shriek, and Tyler braced himself for the impact of her falling body into the water.

"I'm out!" Her tone, descending from above, held hoarse and shaky triumph.

Tyler's heart did a backflip. His girl had done it. Of course she had.

"Go get help."

"Who knows how long that could take? I can't leave you standing in cold water. I'm going to find a way to get you out."

"But if you can't, you have to go."

"I know." Her tone was subdued as if she couldn't bear the thought.

Her footsteps faded from his hearing, and Tyler leaned against the side of the shaft on his good side. Putting his wounded back to the hard rock didn't bear thinking about. Undoubtedly the wounds had started to fester, resulting in the fever that wracked his flesh. Tyler faded into a semiconscious state, barely able to keep himself from crumpling into the water.

A scurry of footsteps brought him back to awareness. A light grew above him—faint, but definitely a soft glow in a very dark place.

"You're not going to believe this." Jen's tone exuded triumph. "They left the rope and lantern at the cave mouth. The lantern's batteries are giving out, but hopefully they'll last long enough to get you out of there."

Soon the rope snaked down into the shaft. Tyler eyed the opportunity for escape with dull eyes.

"I can't climb, Jen. I only have one good hand to grip the rope, and I doubt if I have the strength to pull myself up."

Her face a storm cloud, Jen glared down at him. "You can and you will. I'll help. Now, get a grip—literally."

Obediently, Tyler shuffled over to the rope and wrapped it around his hand several times. "I'll try to walk up the side, but you should stay back. I don't want to pull you in again."

"Stop fussing and climb."

Gritting his teeth, Tyler began the task. His head swam with pain, and his arm shook with weakness, but he refused to release his hold on the rope or cease groping with his feet for foothold after foothold. Yet it seemed his contribution to progress amounted to very little, and her steady hauling on the rope made all the difference. At last he collapsed over the pit's edge onto the cavern floor, a groaning, shivering mass.

Jen knelt beside him. "Come on, mister. There's no rest for you now. We have to get you to civilization and a nice, cushy hospital bed."

Tyler cooperated with her to the best of his ability in getting to his feet, but his efforts were feeble at best. With his arm over her shoulder, they shuffled out of the cavern. He squinted against the bright sunlight piercing his eyes. A headache pulsing through his brain throbbed more intensely.

"One step at a time," Jen told him as they headed down the derelict road.

And that was what they did. The effort strained the limits of his capabilities. How long he'd be able to manage even the measured steps, he didn't know.

"What if Randy and Winthrop are out here waiting to ambush us?" His words emerged a slurred mumble.

"Why would they be? They have no reason to suspect we could escape the tomb they arranged."

Why, indeed? Good question. But then again, what if that assumption was wrong?

FIFTEEN

Jen steeled herself for each forward step. Tyler must be next to passing out, judging by the amount of his weight he leaned onto her. But she could do this. She had to. *They* had to. Together.

The fever heat radiating from his body wound her thoughts into a loop of worry and dread. Might their adversaries be lying in wait as Tyler suggested? She had no extra energy to give to fending them off. Better to lay that anxiety aside and concentrate on what was necessary.

The morning stretched on with the sun climbing toward its zenith. Tyler seemed to rally and take more of his own weight on steadier legs. He didn't waste energy talking, however. Jen bottled up her thoughts and feelings, resisting the urge to tell Tyler she was working on forgiving him, and that she still had feelings for him, but she didn't yet know if those feelings would be enough to get past their years apart or the reason for their separation. Now was not the time to deal with the emotions roiling through her. Finally they reached the fork in the road where they'd fought with Randy and Winthrop.

"I need to sit a minute," Tyler croaked.

His breathing had been growing steadily raspier. It was entirely possible that an infection was settling into his lungs. And who knew what amount of internal injury had been done by the blast of the frag grenade?

Jen lowered him to a seat on a fallen log at the side of the road. Her brows pulled together as she gazed down at his ashen, sweat-dewed face.

"You know you've got to leave me here. I'll be okay until you return with help."

Her heart tore. No, she didn't know he'd be all right that long, because she had no idea how far they were from civilization. There had been no sign of their human adversaries, and that pair possessed no motivation to linger in the woods. But what if a bear came along? There were lots of them in these mountains, and Tyler was too weak to handle a confrontation. And if she had to be gone overnight, other predators roamed. Any medical aide could be too late in getting to him for reasons other than the illness and injuries that currently ravaged him. Nevertheless, Tyler was right. She'd make far better time on her own. Her speed, now, was his best chance.

"I'll be back as quickly as I can."

He lifted his drooping head and managed a smile. "I know. I believe in you."

Yes, he did. He had always been her greatest encourager, especially during those dark days after Mom died and Dad started drowning his sorrows in a bottle. That factor had made Tyler's sudden disappearance from her life all that much more painful and inexplicable. Until now. She knew the truth but hadn't had a spare second to work through the implications or reconcile her emotions.

Later, Jen. Let's do the next needful thing.

Gently, she helped him get as comfortable as possible on the ground leaning up against the log. He could even lie down if he needed to. Then she piled branches and leaves atop him to help his body conserve warmth. Despite the fever, he'd become dangerously chilled in the watery pit, and his clothes were not yet fully dry. Neither were hers.

Jen took off with the stride of a long-distance runner. Her gaze constantly searched her environment and especially the rough terrain passing beneath her feet. She'd be worse than useless to Tyler or herself if she sprained an ankle. The weakness of dehydration challenged her limbs. Her tongue stuck to the roof of her mouth, and her empty stomach tied itself in knots. Still, she refused to slow her pace. With each jarring footfall, she sent up a prayer for deliverance.

When suddenly she burst from the tree line on the verge of a paved road, she stumbled and nearly fell. Heaving for breath, she scanned up and down the narrow, two-lane highway. No traffic was in view, but that could change at any moment. Which way should she go? Impossible to tell from this vantage point what direction would soonest lead to civilization.

The purring of a motor from a vehicle out of sight around a bend took the decision from her. Could the approaching transportation belong to their enemies? The possibility existed, but she didn't dare play it safe and retreat into the trees if there were any chance of flagging down a helpful motorist.

The vehicle swung around the curve into sight. A rattletrap pickup in rust-pocked army green. Waving her arms, Jen sprang forward to the edge of the pavement.

"Help! Someone, please, help!" Her voice emerged in a hoarse croak.

The truck slowed down and came to a stop.

The weathered visage of a bearded oldster peered out at her from the driver's side. The man's dropped jaw and wide eyes telegraphed astonished concern. She must look like a refugee from a cyclone. No matter. Help had arrived.

Sobbing, Jen fell to her knees and gave thanks.

Hours later, Jen gazed out the window of her father's room in the Gatlinburg hospital. She'd come here to wait while Tyler was in surgery. It turned out that their captors had hauled their unconscious bodies more than halfway back to Tennessee from Mount Airy, North Carolina, before veering off into the woods to carry out their macabre and vicious plans. Thus, it made sense to helicopter Tyler to Gatlinburg for medical attention. The chopper had come in over the forest, hovered and lowered a basket to raise his injured body. They'd made room for Jen to ride along, too.

Now it was a waiting game until the doctor reported on Tyler's condition, so she'd come to her father's room to bide her time. Dad was asleep, and he hadn't awakened when she came in. His pale, drawn face and labored breathing—despite the oxygen cannula in his nose—proclaimed clearly enough that the disease ravaging him neared its inevitable culmination that spelled catastrophic loss for her.

She blinked tears away and forced her mind to concentrate on the recent, in-person conversation with Captain Mackey and Tyler's boss, Lamont Jacobs, who'd both been on-site at the hospital when their helicopter landed. The pair had taken her formal statement in a private waiting room. Jacobs had then gone off to circulate Randy's mug shot and the description of Winthrop to all his personnel and make sure Tyler's dogs were cared for. Tyler had mumbled concern about his hound and her pups during the helicopter transport. Mackey had left to put out an all-points bulletin for Randy Givens, along with a description of the man who had masterminded the chaos.

The captain had already gotten back to her with the news that no one by the name of Winthrop, whether it be first or last, was a known associate of Givens. Thus, they remained in the dark about the creepy little guy's full identity or what connection might give him the idea that he stood to inherit the Blackwell emerald mine if other heirs were eliminated. This lack of results was beyond frustrating, particularly when both perpetrators remained on the loose.

Her captain and Tyler's boss seemed to think the pair would be beating feet as far as possible away from the area. Jen remained unconvinced. After all, if they believed her and Tyler to be dead, or as good as, why would they feel the need to flee? No, the threat wasn't over. If and when their adversaries heard their intended victims were very much alive, she didn't doubt they might make another attempt, if only for spite's sake. Winthrop's dreams of inheriting an emerald mine were dead in the water now that his involvement was known, but Randy's vitriol had an unresolved origin.

Dismal reflections to have on her mind. But at least with several bottles of water and a hospital cafeteria meal inside her, as well as a shower and a change of clothes into hospital scrubs, strength was returning, physically and mentally. Woe betide either Randy or Winthrop if they showed up at the hospital.

Still, her anger with those treacherous yahoos who'd been trying to kill her, Tyler and her father were the tip of the iceberg. Resentment simmered against Tyler and her father for abandonment and deception. She was starting to get her head around Tyler's motivations in the mess, and that they'd been altruistic if misguided, but as for Dad—

"Baby girl. You came back." His voice held a phlegmy rasp.

Jen turned to find her father gazing at her.

His hopeful expression wrenched her heart. Her leave-taking after his awful revelations had been anything but pleasant. He had probably wondered if she would ever deign to be in his presence again.

"Of course I did. I may be so angry with you I could spit, but you're still my daddy."

Her father's face folded into deep lines as he frowned. "I should have come clean about everything right away instead of covering up and making Tyler promise to keep my secret."

"Yes, you should have."

His gaze fell away, and he plucked at his blanket with his thumb and forefinger. "It takes a long time…for an alcoholic haze to work its way out of an addict's system. You know I strove toward that, went to meetings…faithfully and all, but still, it took a good while before I had my mind right and could even contemplate confessing to you. By then… Tyler was in the wind with no way to locate him, and you seemed to have your life on track. Digging up the past…felt like it would do more harm than good…so I let things be." He wheezed as he spoke.

"And look how that turned out." Jen plopped heavily into a seat beside his bed.

Her dad raised his eyes to meet hers. "The time was never right before. I know…the situation looks messy right now…but I think it's a God-thing. Bringing you and Tyler together… out of the blue couldn't be anything else."

Jen let out a small, wry laugh. "You might have a point on some level. God does use bad events to bring about good things. Eventually."

"What's the matter?" Her dad jerked his head erect. "Have more attacks happened since you left here a couple of days ago?"

Jen sat forward and told him about the harrowing events at their home in Mount Airy and her and Tyler's trials in the forest and the cave. When she got to the part about meeting Randy and Winthrop face-to-face, her father's breathing grew more labored. She stopped the tale abruptly.

"Should I get the doctor?" Jen gripped her dad's frail hand.

He clamped his fingers tightly around hers. "Winthrop Venner." He practically spat out the name. "He's the worthless deadbeat…who married my sister Tilde and then…ran off as soon as sweet little Cinda…was born with special needs."

Jen sucked in a breath. "That's where I must have heard the unusual name Winthrop before, back so deep in my childhood I only have an impression rather than a clear recollection. But Cinda's mom must have reverted to her maiden name because I don't ever remember Aunt Tilde with the last name Venner." Her father nodded confirmation of the deduction. "Why would this Venner guy think he could inherit the mine?"

"He might think he will have the wealth… at his disposal if he can claim…custody of his perpetually dependent daughter."

Jen scoffed. "Does he think he can successfully challenge the trust fund setup and win guardianship after he abandoned Cinda at birth?"

"Apparently he entertains that hope."

A knock sounded at the door, and a doctor poked his head inside. Not her father's doctor. Tyler's surgeon?

Jen rose, every muscle tensing. "How is he? You can speak in front of us both." She nodded in her father's direction. "We're the nearest thing Tyler has to family."

The truth of that statement jolted through Jen's core. Truly, she hadn't properly appreciated how much Tyler had given up in leaving Mount Airy for her sake the way he had done. She put the realization on the shelf for later examination.

The doctor fully entered the room and smiled. "He's a strong man. We had to remove a considerable quantity of shrapnel from his back, most of which penetrated no further than the dermis of the skin. A few bits were significantly embedded but without organ damage. All wounds were developing an infection, and pneumonia had begun to set into his lungs. We also set the simple fracture of the humerus of his left arm. He'll have some healing time and physical therapy in his future, but he should eventually recover fully."

"That's good news, Doctor." Jen smiled as a great weight she'd hardly realized she was carrying came off her chest. "Thank you."

"That's not my only news." The doctor's smile grew. "Tyler is awake and aware and asking for you, Ms. Blackwell. I told you he's a strong one."

"I'll be right there."

The surgeon gave her Tyler's room number and withdrew.

"I'm coming…with you," her father announced with a cough as soon as the door closed.

"What? No." She glared at him. "You need to stay in bed."

"Bed rest…is overrated." He threw off his covers. "I need…to see Tyler, too."

The man's tone brooked no denial. Clamping her jaw against further protest, Jen left the room to arrange for a wheelchair for the supremely stubborn Jarod Blackwell. The issue of whether it was a wise idea for them both to pop in on Tyler she left in God's hands.

Tyler awoke slowly, aware that he lay on his side to keep pressure off the wounds on his back. A dull ache permeated his body, but painkillers kept the worst of the hurt at bay. They probably also accounted for his inability to remain awake.

He opened his eyes a slit. His pulse jumped, and his eyes popped wide. While he hadn't intended to fall asleep waiting for Jen to show up, he certainly hadn't anticipated his first sight would be her father perched in a wheelchair at his bedside.

"Jarod?" He stared at the man.

Expression sober, Jen's dad lifted a hand in greeting. At least he looked healthier than he had when last Tyler had seen him, though he still wore the nasal cannula. That item would probably be a permanent accessory until the disease ran its course.

Tyler softened his look. "It's good to see you up and about. Where's Jen?"

"I'm here." Her trim figure rounded the bed and came into view.

He drew in a deep breath and let it out slowly. *Thank you, Lord.* She looked hardly the worse for wear after their ordeal, but it was a little odd to see her in scrubs.

"I owe you big-time for getting us both out of that cave and through the woods."

Jen grinned at him. "Don't you forget it, buster. Like I won't forget the several times the past few days that you've saved *me* in the nick of time." She planted her hands on her hips and scanned him up and down. "You still look pretty rough, but I think you might live."

"I think I might." He grinned back at her.

A throat clearing drew both their gazes toward Jarod. The man's eyes glistened with unshed tears.

"Seeing you two together, at last…is the most precious gift of mercy a dying old man could receive." The words came out choked. "I had forgotten the natural flow between you. So rare." He cleared his throat. "My guilt… is almost more than I can stand." Jarod hung his head.

"I forgive you." The words blurted out of Tyler's mouth before he could second-guess them.

Jen's father looked up and met his gaze. "Do you mean that?"

Tyler released a low chuckle. "To my own surprise, I do."

He extended his hand toward the one who had been like a father to him when he was a boy and could be in his heart again. With a soft sob, Jarod gripped Tyler's hand with both of his. Their bony chill and weak squeeze brought home to Tyler the shortness of time on earth remaining to the man. What more needful opportunity to mend broken relationships?

A soft keening came from Jen. Tyler focused on her. Jen's body stood stiff, and her face had gone white as alabaster, her expression stricken. She stood frozen in that pose. Whatever urge she might have to extend forgiveness seemed trapped inside. But her wound was fresh, and she'd had little time to process the information that had turned her world on its axis. Tyler, on the other hand, had known the truth for years, and the offense no longer felt raw. Hopefully time would soothe Jen's heart as well, though, considering Jarod's condition, she had precious little of that commodity.

God, please, help her.

If Jen couldn't or wouldn't choose to forgive—both him and her father—he and Jen had no future. Tyler's heart constricted. What a cruel joke that would be for him and Jen to find each other again only to part forever.

"I've made an appointment...to confess." Jarod's announcement jolted Tyler out of his introspection, and Jen seemed to come to life, her body stiffening.

"What?" She blinked at her father.

"You heard me." Jarod folded his hands together in his lap. "The casino I almost robbed is located in Swain County, North Carolina. A sheriff's deputy from there is coming to see me this afternoon to take my confession. I have no idea if I'll be arrested there and then or not, but I figured you both should know."

Tyler's gaze collided with Jen's.

Clearing her throat, she knelt beside her father's wheelchair. "Have you thought this out, Dad? Why now? What's the point?"

Tyler raised himself on one elbow. "Once Randy is caught, he's likely to spout off about the robbery where his father was killed and proclaim Jarod's involvement."

"That's not why." Jarod's eyes glinted. "Now that I'm not…protecting my daughter from hurtful knowledge… I can't meet my maker… without getting straight with the law. It's…the right thing to do."

Jen turned a wide gaze on Tyler. "What impact will that have on you, do you think? They won't consider you an accessory after the fact?"

Tyler's heart warmed at her instinctive concern for his well-being. "Doubtful. It's so long ago, and there's no proof. Well, other than Jarod's statement."

"And I intend…to keep you out of it, Tyler," the older man said. "You did nothing wrong. Just helped…keep an ornery fool from bleeding to death or dying of…septicemia if you hadn't dug out the bullet. But that detail… doesn't go beyond the three of us."

Tyler shrugged. "It doesn't matter to me either way. I'm pretty sure the county prosecutor will decline to press charges against either of us. Not worth the paperwork, other than to file a notation in the case folder. Nobody but me—and apparently, Freemont's son—had any idea you were ever involved in the first place."

Jen rose to her feet. "Well, then, at least *something* in this mess is getting settled. But I think we're still ignoring the elephant in the room. The people who want all three of us dead are roaming free in the wild."

Tyler tensed. "And when they find out we're all still alive, they will be furious."

"Do you think…we're still in danger?" Jarod's gaze flitted between Tyler and his daughter. "They've been identified and exposed. Randy might…still want his revenge, but—"

"I don't think a little thing like an all-points bulletin will slow them down," Jen interrupted her father. "They've got a sick symbiosis that keeps the mutual goads applied as they try to one-up each other in nastiness. Randy will still crave revenge for his father, and now Winthrop will want revenge, also, for his designs on the mine being thwarted."

Tyler frowned and subsided onto the pillow. "I wish I didn't have to agree with Jen, but I don't believe we can let down our guard. Until these guys are caught, we're going to have to live looking over our shoulders."

His heart sank. Another major impediment to him and Jen exploring a renewal of their relationship. They couldn't relax or think seriously about each other until Jen decided to forgive him and her father and the evil duo was tucked behind bars. Those truths lay bitter on his tongue.

SIXTEEN

Jen drove the familiar route toward the Great Smoky Mountains National Park but didn't take the exit into the park where she used to do her early morning jogs. Sweeping by all park exits, she kept her vehicle pointed toward the address indicated on her dashboard GPS. Tyler's home lay only a few miles away. Her insides fizzed in anticipation of seeing him again. The promised introduction to his coonhound and her seven-week-old pups and being welcomed into his home for the first time were side benefits.

A week had passed since their kidnapping and harrowing misadventure at the hands of the crooked pair who remained on the loose. Yet they all had lots to be thankful for. Tyler's prediction about the lack of interest in prosecuting anyone for the long-ago attempted casino robbery had proven correct. Dad had gotten strong enough to return to his care home, and Tyler had been released from the hospital the day after he'd gone in.

Since then, Jen and Tyler hadn't seen each other, though they'd spoken daily on the phone. They had both been busy resuming their lives—Tyler recuperating at home, and Jen finally starting her new job with the Gatlinburg Police Department. So far, she loved it, except for that constant niggle in the back of her mind that hostile eyes could be watching her. But so far, no sightings of Randy or Winthrop had been reported.

Could she and Tyler be mistaken in believing those guys wouldn't give up their vendetta, and was the evil pair instead far away from Tennessee? If so, a case could be made that the men were getting their revenge by forcing her, her father and Tyler to live on edge daily for no reason.

If Jen were honest with herself, she was on edge for an additional reason. Anger toward her father lingered. She hadn't yet been able to utter the words, "I forgive you," though she spent time with him daily. What sort of a hypocrite was she to keep on hiding her simmering feelings beneath a veneer of kindness? Yet how could she act anything but kind toward a dying man—a father who had raised her and made all sorts of sacrifices for her well-being throughout her childhood? Somehow knowing those things and the closeness of their relationship made it harder rather than easier to forgive the staggering deception that had cast Tyler out of her life.

God, help me. Without divine intervention, she might not be capable of fulfilling a required element of the Christian life—forgive as one has been forgiven. What was the matter with her? If only she knew.

The turn came up on the left, and Jen thrust her inner struggle back down into the dark box where she kept it. She signaled and guided her vehicle into a gravel-topped driveway flanked by forest on either side. The house didn't come into view until at least a hundred yards had crunched beneath her tires. Then the woods opened into a spacious clearing. A single-story, log cabin–type home with a pair of dormers and an attached garage took up nearly a third of the area. A lush, neatly trimmed yard occupied the rest of what must be a good acre of cleared land. A wide porch spanned the front of the home and hosted a two-seater swing, as well as a pair of rockers next to a low table.

Jen pulled up in front of the house and stopped her car yet remained inside the vehicle observing details of the property. Before he was injured, Tyler must have planted the neat beds of pansies and baby's breath that fronted the porch on either side of the steps. A water feature with a bubbling fountain anchored the space to the right of a sidewalk leading to the home, and a spreading maple tree anchored the space to the left.

What was missing?

No tall figure stepping out the front door to greet her, for one thing. And no dog barking at the arrival of a stranger. Not that Tyler *had* to trot outside and welcome her. She was perfectly capable of going to the door and knocking. The dog wouldn't necessarily bark, either. Maybe Tyler had trained it not to create a ruckus for visitors. The prickles on the back of her neck probably had no other foundation than the hypervigilance permeating her every waking moment.

Grabbing her handbag with one hand, Jen opened her car door with the other and stepped outside. Odors of recently trimmed grass— naughty Tyler for potentially overexerting himself—and the nearby pine trees filled her nostrils. A balmy breeze caressed her bare arms showing beneath her short-sleeved blouse. In such peaceful surroundings, why was her stomach knotting?

Her hand delved into her purse and closed around the butt of the handgun she carried everywhere, even off duty. She could feel foolish later, when all was shown to be well, but for now she'd err on the side of caution. Then she trod up the sidewalk and the steps to the front door.

No doorbell presented itself, but a rustic knocker held pride of place in the middle of the door panel. She gave the metal a pair of raps. No voice answered her, but the knob turned from the inside, and the door swung noiselessly open to reveal a spacious foyer. No one stood directly inside the door. If only she could say that detail remained the only anomaly.

Several feet away, Tyler sat with a rope around his torso binding him to a dining table armchair. His left arm sported a bent-elbowed cast from below his shoulder to above his wrist. A wide piece of duct tape covered his mouth, but his fierce gaze broadcasted fury. Not because of her arrival, but due to the scowling, lanky man standing behind him and holding a gun to his head. Every hair on Jen's body stood on end, and her hand tightened around her gun butt.

"Ah, ah, ah!" admonished a beaming Winthrop as he stepped out from behind the open door panel. "Bring your hand out of your purse slowly, and it better be empty."

Gritting her teeth, Jen complied.

"Get in here." Randy's dead-cold tone sent a shiver up her spine, but she suppressed any outward sign of her reaction. "We have unfinished business."

"We certainly do." Steeling herself, Jen stepped smoothly over the threshold. "It's called putting you two in prison where you belong."

"Wrong!" Randy snarled. "Prison is where your daddy belongs. And this guy, too." He rapped Tyler on the top of the head with his gun barrel.

"I guess you haven't gotten the memo. The Swain County district attorney has declined to prosecute."

"Yeah? Well, we haven't. I'm going to—"

"That's enough!" Winthrop's words lashed the air, and Randy paused in the act of raising his gun toward Jen. "Let's keep things civil until our business is completed."

"Business?" Jen turned her head toward the grinning little man.

Winthrop motioned her to precede him into the cozy living room to the right. On a rustic wooden coffee table sat a laptop with its lid open. "Have a seat on the sofa in front of the computer."

On reluctant feet, Jen trod toward the coffee table. "What do you want?"

"Sit down, and I'll tell you."

"Tell me now, or I'm not making another move."

Winthrop heaved a great sigh as if highly put upon. "During Randy's a bit too zealous interrogation of the financial advisor with the frail heart, the man told him you have a sizable account in your name—a percentage of the proceeds from the Blackwell emerald mine. I need you to transfer those funds in their entirety to the account number I will give you. Then we can leave you in peace. Permanently."

Jen whirled with a scowl toward the officious crook. "If you're going to kill us anyway, what incentive do I have to give you my money?"

Randy let out a snarl. "The incentive that I'll put a bullet in your boyfriend's head right now if you don't."

Jen's shoulders slumped, and she turned toward the laptop.

"I'll take that." Winthrop reached for her purse even as Jen caught Tyler's sudden move out of the corner of her eye.

He threw his entire chair sideways and fell to the floor with it. Jen reacted instantly, slinging her gun-weighted purse by the long strap directly at Winthrop's head. The man staggered and went down with a loud grunt.

Randy gaped, standing frozen and wide-eyed as a deer in the headlights, as if he didn't know whom to shoot first, her or Tyler. The shock lasted but a split second, and he was leveling his gun toward Jen. She dove behind the meager cover of the coffee table while scrabbling for her own pistol. There was no way she would get the gun free before a bullet spat her way.

But then from his seemingly helpless position on the floor, Tyler swiveled his hips and rammed his legs, chair and all, into Randy's lower body. The man's gun blasted as he flipped top over tail, landing flat on his back on the foyer's hardwood floor. He rolled and attempted to stand up, but Jen was already on him with a kick to the hand that sent the gun flying out of his grip, followed by a second kick to his face that laid him back down flat, eyes rolling in his head.

Jen took up a firing stance that gave her a clear shot at both groggy targets. "Randy Givens and Winthrop Venner, you're under arrest for murder, attempted murder, kidnapping and a host of offenses to be named in your indictments."

She spared a glance down at Tyler. His smile was masked behind the tape, but his eyes glowed approval.

* * *

Three days later, Tyler ruffled Dixie's floppy ears and let her out into the fenced-in run in his backyard. She appeared healthy, all the wooziness from the sedative Randy had given her the day they ambushed him at his house completely out of her system. The louse claimed to have a soft spot for good hunting dogs and expected Tyler to thank him for not allowing Winthrop to simply put a bullet in her. Yes, Tyler was intensely grateful his dog had not been shot, but he owed bad actors nothing for showing minimal restraint. He'd been forced to wean the puppies sooner than he liked because he didn't want them nursing on milk tainted by drugs. Thankfully that process was going well, also.

Randy and Winthrop were being held without bail, and Tyler confidently expected them to reap maximum sentences with no possibility of parole. Though never arrested before, Winthrop turned out to have quite the background as a suspect in over three decades' worth of criminal activities facilitating drug and weapons deals. These connections had made the pair extraordinarily dangerous, with the older man's access to non-civilian items like the explosives they'd used in their attacks. Thanks to Jen, the guys were now removed from society, and he, Jen and Jarod could breathe easy.

Tyler's cell phone rang, and he pulled it from his belt holder. The screen said Jen was calling. His pulse thrummed faster, and a grin broke out on his face. He answered the call, and his grin faded as she spoke.

A brief car ride later, he strode up the hallway of Jarod's care home toward the man's room. His heart hung heavy in his chest. Jen had called him to say the end was near, and her father wanted them both beside him. If only they had more time to say proper goodbyes. He would have enjoyed more conversations with Jarod now that the slate was clean between them. Then again, no time was enough for loved ones during this pivotal transition.

Please, God, let there be an opportunity for Jen to make peace with her father, and help her to take advantage of Your grace.

Tyler slowed as he approached the door that stood slightly ajar. Voices, though not the sense of the words, carried to him. He stopped on the threshold. The tone of the conversation felt weighty. Should he knock? Something stopped him with his fist poised to rap on the wood.

"No, Dad." Jen's tone was harsh. "I won't pretend your choices haven't scarred me for life."

Tyler's gut clenched as Jarod murmured a response he couldn't decipher. But apparently, based on Jen's statement, Tyler wouldn't receive an affirmative answer to his prayer. His heart grieved for Jen as much as for her father. Was there anything he could do? Not really. Yielding to the Holy Spirit's prompting to forgive was Jen's choice and hers alone.

A gusty sigh from Jen reached Tyler's ears. As if she were breathing out all her angst.

"But God can make our wounded places our strongest places." Her voice had lost its rough edge and had become firm and confident. "God's forgiven you, so of course, I forgive you, Daddy. You've paid for your mistake with much heartache, just as Tyler and I have. It's time to put the past in the past."

Tyler's heart leaped. A smile spread his lips as he knocked softly on the door.

"Come in," Jen called.

He entered the sitting room. Jarod lay semi-prone in a recliner with a blanket covering his frail frame.

The man grinned at him, eyes sparkling in a gaunt face. "Did…you hear?"

Heat crept up Tyler's neck. "I shouldn't have been eavesdropping, but a part of me doesn't truly regret the transgression."

Jen smirked from her seat at her father's side.

"Since I'm in a forgiving mood, I shall pardon you, also. Both for listening in on a private conversation and for keeping secrets."

"Thank you." The simple statement bore a freight load of meaning.

Her nod said she understood. Like she always did.

Jarod motioned for Tyler to take a seat next to Jen. He didn't hesitate to comply. Jen took Tyler's right hand in hers, and Jarod laid a palm on his cast.

"What a bunch we are." Jen smiled.

Tyler returned her smile. "I think they call it a family."

Jarod nodded without a word. By the wheeze of his breathing, he seemed nearly beyond speech, but then the man proved Tyler wrong.

"I need…one…more…thing."

"What is it, Dad?" Jen leaned close to her father.

The man moved his eyes from his daughter to Tyler and back again.

"You need me and Jen to tell each other how we feel?"

Jarod nodded with vigor.

"Okay." Tyler turned toward Jen and gazed into her eyes. Lips slightly parted, she looked back at him. "I love you, Jennifer Blackwell.

I always have, and I always will. There is no one else for me but you."

A tear made a moist track down her blushing cheek. "Tyler Cade, I've been in love with you since the first time I called you Tyger because I couldn't pronounce my *l*'s. And that has never changed and never will."

The backs of Tyler's eyes stung, but he held the tears back as he leaned forward and gently pressed his lips to Jen's. The warm taste of her was sweeter even than he remembered.

"Those vows…are…good enough…for me."

He and Jen turned toward her father.

Peace radiated from the man's face as he closed his eyes. Jarod never opened them again or said another word until he gently passed in the wee hours of the morning. Tyler and Jen never left his side—or each other's.

EPILOGUE

Six months later

Jen stared into the mirror and for a fleeting moment missed her father terribly. Then she pushed the sadness away. Daddy might not be here in the flesh to walk her down the aisle, but today was for joy and nothing else.

In sync with Jen's thought, her beaming matron of honor—an old friend from the Memphis PD—came up behind her and fitted the demure, lacy half-veil over Jen's professional style that had turned her dense blond hair into an intricate coronet offset by freestanding curls.

"You look *gorgeous*." The brunette woman fussed with the hang of the bridal gown's understated train. "Tyler is going to be knocked off his feet. I hope he doesn't make a total fool of himself and literally faint at the altar."

The women grinned at each other, and the

other three bridal attendants laughed aloud. One of them was Rachel Tarrant, Tyler's colleague in the park ranger service. Jen had been nervous that the woman's aspirations toward Tyler would create a problem with jealousy, but Rachel had taken the news of Tyler's engagement to Jen quite well. The explanation became obvious when Tyler informed her that his colleague had met someone else.

A knock sounded at the door, but it didn't open.

"It's time," said an usher's voice.

Amid muted chatter and soft giggles, the wedding party made their way to the church foyer to meet up with the groomsmen. Jen lagged behind them, staying out of sight of the low stage at the front of the church, though she could still see the first three-quarters of the aisle. She and Tyler had decided to be old-fashioned and delay the picture-taking until after the wedding so the groom didn't get to see the bride before the ceremony.

The music changed, and the little flower girl and ring bearer began to walk up the aisle. To be honest, the progression shaped up to be more of a scamper than a stately progress. Jen stifled a smile. Then the attendants began to take their cues and move with measured tread toward the stage.

At last, the traditional bridal march swelled. Taking in a deep breath and letting it out slowly, Jen stepped into full view of everyone in the sanctuary. All eyes fastened on her, but she had eyes for only one.

Jen's gaze locked with Tyler's. His jaw dropped and his eyes widened, but rather than going pale, his face flushed with healthy color. Every nuance of his body language cried, *Welcome, my love.*

Though Jen moved down the aisle singly, her satin skirt swishing, she had no sense of being alone. In a break with tradition, Jen had nixed the idea of finding a substitute for her father to make this walk with her. Her daddy accompanied her in her heart.

Tyler's fixed gaze drew Jen like true north on a compass. As if the white slippers on her feet had turned to air, every floating step took her closer to the fulfillment of a lifelong dream and the start of a new adventure where she and Tyler walked hand in hand wherever this unpredictable thing called life would take them.

* * * * *

If you liked this story from Jill Elizabeth Nelson, check out some of her previous Love Inspired Suspense books,

Lone Survivor
The Baby's Defender
Hunted for Christmas
In Need of Protection
Unsolved Abduction
Hunted in Alaska
Safeguarding the Baby

Available from Love Inspired Suspense!

Find more great reads at www.LoveInspired.com.

Dear Reader,

Thank you for traveling with Jen and Tyler on this difficult path through abandonment, betrayal and reconciliation, not to mention the constant danger from unseen enemies. Have you ever suddenly run into someone you haven't seen in years but who used to mean something to you? How did you feel—especially if the separation was difficult or unexplained? If you've had the experience, you may be able to relate well to Jen's struggle with abandonment. Have you ever discovered dark secrets lurking in someone you loved and revered? If so, you should be able to understand Jen and Tyler's struggles with forgiveness. I hope my characters' challenges and triumphs have ministered to you.

I enjoy hearing from my readers. My email address is jnelson@jillelizabethnelson.com, and my website is http://jillelizabethnelson.com. I am also available to contact through my Facebook page: https://www.facebook.com/JillElizabethNelson.Author.

Blessings,
Jill Elizabeth Nelson

75TH ANNIVERSARY

LOVE INSPIRED SUSPENSE
INSPIRATIONAL ROMANCE

Caught in a murderer's crosshairs...
Secrets can be lethal.

After discovering a dead body in Great Smoky Mountains National Park, Detective Jen Blackwell is ambushed—until federal park ranger Tyler Cade comes to the rescue. And when the culprit sets their sights on Jen's father, it's clear that someone is targeting them. She has no choice but to team up with her ex-boyfriend. Only Tyler's hiding something...and old secrets could cost them their lives.

CATEGORY: **SUSPENSE**

$7.99 U.S./$8.99 CAN.

ISBN-13: 978-1-335-59933-9

50799

EAN

9 781335 599339

S

Courage.
Danger.
Faith.

LOVE INSPIRED
LoveInspired.com